EARTH'S TRIANGLE
EARTH'S MAGIC
BOOK SIX

EVE LANGLAIS

Earth's Triangle © 2023 Eve Langlais

Cover by Addictive Covers © 2023

Produced in Canada

Published by Eve Langlais

http://www.EveLanglais.com

E-ISBN: 978 177 384 4848

Print ISBN: 978 177 384 4855

ALL RIGHTS RESERVED

This book is a work of fiction and the characters, events and dialogue found within the story are of the author's imagination and are not to be construed as real. Any resemblance to actual events or persons, either living or deceased, is completely coincidental.

No part of this book may be reproduced or shared in any form or by any means, electronic or mechanical, including but not limited to digital copying, AI training, file sharing, audio recording, email and printing without permission in writing from the author.

PROLOGUE

The witch, wearing a long flowing cloak with the hood up, keeping her face in shadow, left her cottage, a woven basket hung over her arm.

A watching Ambrose and Orion glanced at each other and grinned. Now was their chance.

The young boys, one pale of skin with golden hair, and the other his opposite with ebony skin and dark crown, crept down from the tree boughs, careful to not snap any twigs or rustle leaves. People claimed witches could set spells to listen for intruders. They also muttered about how the spell-casting hags kept treasure troves hidden in their abodes. A wealth two orphaned boys could use to fill their hungry bellies.

Orion sauntered without a care across the tended cobble path to the front door, but Ambrose hesitated. A prickle on his nape led to him glancing behind at the forest. The witch should be long gone, yet a sudden disquiet had him whispering, "Maybe this ain't such a good idea."

Orion paused on the threshold of the house to peer back at him over his shoulder. "Don't be a yellow belly. T'will be simple. We go in, grab a few things, and leave. She'll probably not even notice."

"I'd notice if it was my things being stolen," Ambrose insisted.

"That's 'cause you don't have much but the clothes on your back. You'd get cold right quick if you was naked," Orion said with a snicker.

"Bloody death tax. Took everything," grumbled Ambrose.

When the pox took his parents, it left him with nothing. His home, his few belongings, all seized by the tax man and him tossed to the streets to fend for himself. Alone and afraid, Ambrose spent those first few days in misery, huddled in alleys, scrounging for scraps. It was how Orion found him.

The same age as Ambrose, Orion knew how to survive and taught Ambrose. Begging for coins or food. Stealing a bite to eat when vendors had their backs turned. Not exactly how Ambrose wanted to live, but starvation had a way of changing a boy's morals.

"I'm going in. You coming?" Orion asked as he pushed open the door.

"Yeah." As Ambrose shuffled to join his friend, he couldn't help glancing around, still convinced someone watched.

The inside of the cottage proved as rustic as the

exterior, but tidy. Fragrant herbs hung in bunches from the rafters. A stone hearth showed wood piled and ready for lighting. A pot hung from a hook over it. A table took up the most room and held a basket full of fruit.

Orion snagged an apple and bit in, the crispy crunch almost as appetizing as the juices that ran down his chin. Ambrose almost drooled.

"Delicious! Have one." Orion tossed him an apple.

Ambrose caught it but didn't eat it. He eyed his friend and said, "Whatcha think the witch'll do to us if she catches us stealing?"

"She won't catch us," a confident Orion stated.

"What if she turns us into frogs or something?" He remembered it happening in a story his mother used to recite to him before bed.

"Then we'll have plenty of flies to eat." Orion poked out his tongue comically before taking another juicy bite.

Ambrose couldn't resist. He crunched into his apple and groaned at the sweet, crisp taste.

"I'm going to grab some for later." Orion stuffed two apples into his pockets, plus a pair of plums. Fruit that should have been out of season. How did the witch get them?

"She doesn't look rich," Ambrose noted as he ate his treat.

"That's 'cause she hides it. It's probably under the floor."

"It's dirt."

Orion frowned. "Maybe in the ceiling." They craned to look upward, but only herbs hung.

"We should leave. Those apples will tide us over until tomorrow."

"Not yet." Orion moved to the bed and the chest at the foot of it. He flipped open the lid to show folded garments and linens. He rifled through the pile before exclaiming, "Aha." He held up a picture frame, the edges of it gilded. Probably valuable.

Ambrose moved closer and gazed at the photo within, a recent thing that he didn't quite like, seeing as how he didn't understand how a box could spit out an image. Had to be magic. The picture was of the witch, recognizable by her beaked nose, but younger. She had her arm around a girl about their age with the same feature. A daughter most likely.

"I didn't know the witch had a child," Ambrose mused. Everyone stated she lived alone.

A subdued Orion murmured, "I saw a grave in the garden."

"Oh." For some reason, it made Ambrose sad. He knew what it felt like to lose someone close. Before he could say anything, Orion stuffed the picture frame back into the chest and slammed the lid shut.

"You're right. There's nothing here. Let's go."

It relieved Ambrose to hear that. Was it wrong to take a few pieces of fruit? Yes, but taking a memory? That would have truly been terrible.

As they whirled to head for the door, it opened, and the witch stood framed.

Both boys froze, mouths agape.

"Hello," she said softly.

"Um..." Orion appeared at a loss for words.

Whereas Ambrose blabbered, "We're sorry. We was hungry and had an apple."

"We can't give back the ones we ate, but here's the stuff we took for later." Orion emptied his pockets without prompting.

The witch pushed back her hood to show a face lined with age, her hair gray and tied back, her eyes intense and a strange mauve color.

"Do not apologize for eating because you're hungry. Thank you, though, for not taking the only picture I have of my daughter."

"We don't want to be thieves," Ambrose blurted out. "But no one will hire us on account we're too young."

"It's a crime how they treat orphans in this town." The witch shook her head. "And I can sense you have good hearts. I know someone who is looking for boys such as you. Hard-working lads to do special tasks."

"What kind of tasks?" Orion asked suspiciously, with good reason. There'd been a gent who'd offered to hire them but had been vague about the details. It turned out he'd wanted to use them in a way no young boy should ever be used. They'd escaped, but the close call left them leery.

As if she'd read their minds, the witch shook her head. "Never would my goddess abuse the innocent."

"Which goddess do you serve?" Ambrose's parents

hadn't been very religious. They went to church every Sunday, but they'd not been true believers like some.

"I serve the Goddess Hekate. Have you heard of her?"

Orion shook his head, but Ambrose knew. "She is the goddess of magic. Why would she need us?"

"Because not everyone can hear her voice. How would you feel about being her messengers?"

"What's it pay?" Orion got to the crux of it.

"Enough for you to have a bed every night to sleep in. Food in your belly. Proper clothing instead of rags."

"Is it dangerous?" Ambrose blurted out because it sounded too good to be true.

"At times it might be. As her messengers, you might have to travel to perilous locations."

"Can't travel far on two feet," Orion pointed out.

"A good thing that transportation will be provided," the witch stated with a smile. "To start, you'll travel by carriage or train, but as you grow, should you stay in her service, then you'll have to learn to ride."

"I'd get to ride a horse!" Ambrose had always loved them but only ever sat on a pony once at a fair.

"Yes, a horse," the witch laughed in reply. "What say you, Orion and Ambrose?"

Rather than ask how she knew their name, they nodded, and Orion solemnly stated, "We accept."

From that day forward, they never went hungry again. On the contrary, they thrived and proved themselves worthy servants. They eventually became known as Hekate's hounds, her scions on Earth.

CHAPTER 1

"She sure is cute," Orion stated, eyeing the woman with voluptuous curves as she entered a store across the street.

"You should know better than to use the C word," Ambrose chided.

"Can't say cute, can't say hot, can't say holy fucking boner. These modern times suck," Orion pouted.

"It's called evolution," Ambrose stated, sounding pompous. His close friend of the past century liked to think himself a scholar and read all kinds of stuffy magazines and books. Orion preferred to be in the moment. And in that moment, he really admired the woman they'd been sent to observe. A week now, and he tired of simply watching.

"Evolution is us crawling from the sea. Making perfectly good words bad is just annoying," Orion grumbled under his breath. But his discontent didn't last long. "Isn't it time we introduced ourselves?"

"Most definitely not. Our goddess tasked us with watching over the human. It will be easier if we do so from afar." Their goddess being Hekate, the deity of magic. They'd been her scions ever since she took them under her wing. Best decision ever.

"Watch for what exactly?" Their instructions hadn't been clear. They'd received the mission in the form of a mental message that simply showed them an image of the woman, her location, and the instruction to protect if necessary. Nothing more.

Given they were obedient hounds, they'd hopped a plane to Montreal and located the woman in question, who lived in a tiny basement apartment with its windows barred. They'd followed her every morning for the past week as she went to her job in a tiny sandwich shop.

While Hekate had indicated the female was human, Orion had given her trail a good sniff to make sure. Sometimes their goddess didn't provide all the details when she sent them on a mission. It should be noted she didn't get involved often in Earthly or human affairs. Although, of late, they'd had back-to-back tasks. Blame the fact times were a-changing.

Old gods had woken. Battles had been fought. The arcane was becoming more prevalent everywhere you looked, except where this woman was concerned.

Name Adeline Gagnon, age thirty-nine. Single. Never married. Had two cats—an unfortunate choice since everyone knew dogs were much better. No kids. No living family that they'd found. No car, or debt. From what they could see, this woman woke up, went to work at the sandwich shop where she'd been employed for the last eighteen years, went home. Rinse, repeat.

Nothing about her drew attention, unless her bodacious bod counted. According to her driver's license record—which Ambrose acquired via the dark web—she stood five foot nine, a hundred and eighty-five pounds. She kept her dark hair in a short bob and wore thick, black-rimmed glasses but eschewed makeup. Not that she needed any. Her clear complexion accentuated her high cheekbones and full lips.

On a whim, Orion pushed up from the park bench they'd commandeered. For cover, they each had a newspaper and a coffee—large Tim Horton's paper cups that offered "Roll Up the Rim" prizes via an app. An app! Kind of defeated the whole roll-up part. It especially sucked since he lost while Ambrose won a free donut. The man didn't even like sweets.

Inactivity made Orion restless, hence why he dumped the paper and his cup into the trash and slicked back his hair.

"Where are you going?" Ambrose asked, folding his paper to fix him with a stern eye.

"I am getting myself a sandwich."

"I thought we were going to watch and not interact."

"That was your plan, and it's bor-r-ring," Orion whined. "Besides, I'm hungry, and it just so happens she makes sandwiches. I would add it's also probably a good idea to get a peek inside her place of work. Get a good sniff too, you know, in case there's some funky shit going on out of sight."

"Please. We both know you're going in to flirt with her," Ambrose accused.

"Is it flirting if it's just my natural outgoing personality?"

The reply had Ambrose rolling his eyes. "Not every woman has to be a conquest."

"Excuse me, but I do not try and seduce every female I meet."

"And yet they end up in your bed," Ambrose's dry reply.

"Not my fault they find me attractive and drop their panties begging me for some loving." A bit of an exaggeration. They didn't beg. They simply threw themselves at him, and he didn't want to be rude.

"You're a whore, Orion." Ambrose shook his head.

"And you're uptight, old friend. I can't wait for the day when you meet a woman who manages to loosen you up and leave you spinning."

"As if I'd ever match with someone chaotic."

"You know what they say. Opposites attract."

"Does this mean you're going to end up with a sweet and sensible girl who isn't impressed by your charm and expects you to take out the garbage?"

"Perish the thought. I'm never settling down."

Orion declared it, mostly because he'd been saying it for the past century. He wasn't about to admit that, of late, the freewheeling lifestyle of a bachelor had finally begun to wear on him. Different faces every other night. The same vapid conversations. Pleasure quick and fleeting, forgotten the moment it was done.

He blamed his retrospect on having been in close proximity to a couple newly in love. Seeing how Marissa and Koda eyed each other, the way they'd eagerly rushed off every time they got a chance to be intimate, the secret smiles they shared… It all aroused a feeling in him that he didn't often feel.

Envy.

Weird. Probably just a passing phase.

"Want anything?" he asked Ambrose as he stood on the curb, waiting for a car to pass.

"Since you insist on going in, then yes. Ham and cheese on rye, light on the mustard—"

"Hold the pickle, no lettuce, but yes to bacon if they have some. I know." Ambrose never deviated. "You know, you should expand your horizons. Try something new."

"I could say the same about you."

"What are you talking about? I'm always up for new experiences," Orion boasted.

"Says the man who has never had a real girlfriend and cringes at the idea of monogamy."

"And deprive the world of my skills as a lover? Perish the thought," Orion declared as he crossed the street.

The sandwich shop sat between an appliance repair store and a tarot reader. The sign above the shop, a simple plank of painted wood, stated, *Sandwiches Your Way*. It didn't have any gimmicks or flashy lights. Probably explained the light foot traffic they'd observed this past week. These days people wanted an experience they could post on social media. The lack of business could also be because the food sucked. He'd soon find out.

A bell tinkled as he entered. The scent of cured meat and freshly baked bread filled his nostrils, along with a hint of his target's lingering perfume—his target, who didn't stand behind the counter. No one did. Not really a surprise since they never saw any other employees entering the place. Could be they did so via the alley, but the few times Orion posted himself to watch, he'd only ever seen Adeline popping out for a breath of air.

Orion stood before the glass display that held hunks of meat, ready to be sliced. The board on the wall behind listed the day's special—tuna club on a pretzel roll—along with a list of basic sandwiches. Roast beef, ham, pastrami, meatball. There was also a mix-and-match option where all the types of breads and toppings were listed for someone to build themselves an epic sandwich a la Shaggy and Scooby-Doo.

The beaded curtain leading to the back room rustled as a woman emerged. His target. Adeline Gagnon. She looked even more delicious up close.

Orion beamed her with his gazillion-watt, panty-dropping smile. "Well, hello there."

She remained smooth-featured and said, "How can I help you, sir?"

Sir. Ack. He almost grimaced. "Looking for two sandwiches. A boring ham and cheese on rye for my friend, no lettuce or pickle, easy on the mustard, with bacon, please."

She immediately began pulling out a fresh loaf of rye and sliced it. As she piled on the fixings, she asked, "And for you, sir?"

"What do you suggest, sweetheart?"

Despite the flirty term, she didn't look up or even blush. Most likely she had strange men complimenting her day in and out. But still, Orion wasn't used to women ignoring him.

"Our special of the day is a good choice."

His lips twisted. "I'll be honest, I'm more of a beef than fish kind of guy."

"Then might I suggest the roast beef au jus, on a fresh baguette, topped with sauteed mushrooms, provolone cheese, and a hint of horseradish."

"That sounds delicious."

She finished wrapping the first sandwich and began work on his, not once looking at him or engaging. Probably shy.

"So what's your favorite sandwich?" he asked.

"I don't eat bread," she remarked. "Or meat for that matter."

He blinked in surprise. "But you work in a deli shop."

"I do."

"Wouldn't you prefer to work somewhere you don't have to deal with stuff you don't like?"

She cast him a brief glance. "I don't like a lot of things. Not a reason to steer clear of them. Besides, this way it's easier to avoid temptation. I worked in an ice cream shop before this. Not a good idea since I've a weakness for cookie dough chocolate chip."

Aha, she had a sweet tooth.

Before he could draw out some more info, she presented him with the sandwiches. "That will be forty-two seventy-one."

His jaw almost dropped. "For two sandwiches?"

"Two very good sandwiches," she firmly stated.

He had the cash, but still... The pricing explained the lack of customers. He counted out forty-three dollars and handed it over. She offered him the change, which he dumped into the tip jar and added another five. Forty-eight bucks for two sandwiches. They'd better be the best he'd ever eaten.

Orion snared the paper bag she'd put them in, and before he could say another word, she disappeared into the back.

Not very social. He returned to Ambrose with the food, a bemused expression leading his friend to say, "What happened?"

"I just got fleeced. Do you know how much I paid for these?" He shook the bag. Although, one bite later, he did have to admit it was the best damned sandwich he'd ever eaten.

Pity hardly anyone entered the shop to find out. Some went in and quickly left empty-handed. A few went inside and stayed in there so long he had to wonder what was going on. The window had a glare that didn't let him see in. Those men—and only men, he noticed—eventually exited with a bag that he assumed held a sandwich.

The shop closed at six, and they trailed Adeline home. She carried only her purse and never once looked back.

Never saw the wererat trailing her.

But the hounds did.

Orion almost sighed with relief. At last, their boring job was about to get interesting.

CHAPTER 2

Adeline entered her basement apartment and kicked off her shoes with a sigh. Nothing like being barefoot after a day's work.

"Hey, Smudge and Fudge." She greeted her cats lying on the slim ledge of the basement window. The pair stretched, and each opened an eye to peek at her then promptly went back to sleep.

Par for the course. At times she wondered why she fed them. A male and female Siamese with vivid blue eyes she'd found in the alley behind the shop wearing matching collars. She'd tried to drop them off at the local animal shelter, only they were full. Adeline had no choice but to take them home, however, she did her due diligence and put-up flyers. No one ever replied. She wasn't exactly upset given she found herself loving the cute pair. Next thing she knew, she'd bought all the supplies needed; bed, cat tower and toys, fancy food—only to have them eschew everything feline. They preferred fresh fish, never played with toys—unless the occasional rodent or large spider counted—and slept either in the window or on her pillow, usually after nudging her from it.

At times she wondered why they stayed, seeing how they barely paid her any mind. That didn't stop her from trying to earn their affection.

She padded over to her tiny kitchenette with its bar-sized fridge. The fresh can of tuna she pulled from the cupboard brought them trotting, and Smudge even rubbed against her leg for a quick second before she shoved her face into the bowl to chomp. Adeline chose to have salad with lentils for dinner and peaches with cream for dessert.

After she did her few dishes, she turned on the television and half-watched it while sweeping up cat hair. So much hair.

With her small place clean, she sat on her pull-out couch, which doubled as her bed, and sighed. Busy day today. The shop's high prices hadn't deterred a few clients, and so she'd actually had to make sandwiches. Ugh. Not her favorite thing, to be honest. She'd not lied when she told that one client, the good-looking blond, that she didn't do bread or meat.

Vegetarian all the way. Cheese and eggs were her only animal products, and they were ethically sourced, imported from a farm in Nexus. Annie, the owner, delivered monthly.

At ten, Adeline pulled out her bed from the couch and slept for a few hours until a low growl woke her.

"What is it, kitties?" she murmured, rolling onto her back.

Rowr. One of her cats didn't sound happy. Understandable, given she blinked sleep from her eyes to see the ungodly time of two fifty-three a.m.

Sigh. And she had to be up by five.

She swung her legs over the side of the bed as her cats continued to make noise. "I know. I know. Someone's at the door. Give me a second." She reached under the bed and pulled out the taser, freshly charged since the last incident. In her other hand, she held a baseball bat. Good for whacking and less messy than a knife.

Armed, she then planted herself in front of the door and waited.

The knob turned, left, then right, squeaking on purpose. She didn't oil it because she wanted to hear when someone tried to break in on the off-chance one day her kitties decided to not warn her. Who knew cats would make such good guards?

She didn't turn on a light. She knew from experience it wouldn't deter. She waited.

Click.

Her locks never seemed to foil those picking them. And she'd tried. Mega deadbolts. Electronic ones. Specialized custom keys. Even the magically hexed versions failed. It became easier to just let them come in.

The door opened, and there it stood, about four

feet tall, its nose pink, like the tip of its tail, with red eyes and whiskers.

A wererat. Not her first.

It hissed and showed yellowed teeth.

"Yeah, yeah, you're vicious," she grumbled. "Let's get this over with."

Before she could dart in and zap it with the taser, a low growl—not of the feline variety—preceded a large dog pouncing the wererat from behind. The first creature uttered a piercing noise of rage as it hit the floor, buried under a massive, black-furred hound. The two began to tussle, with the wererat managing to scramble free. The dog advanced on it, drawing it deeper into the tiny apartment. Not good. While she didn't own much of worth, she'd scrimped for the television and would hate to have to replace it.

The cats jumped to the windowsill and watched with flicking tails as the dog feinted toward the wererat, which swiped with its clawed paw. The big furball lunged and took the wererat to the floor. A chomp to the neck and a crunch of bone led to the wererat going limp.

One down.

The winner looked at Adeline, its eyes unnaturally bright. This was no ordinary dog. Just freaking lovely.

Her cats uttered a low warning growl. Another threat according to them, despite the fact it took out the monster. All she needed to know. Adeline darted forward, taser in hand, and zapped it.

The dog gave her a look of betrayal as its body

jiggled. But it didn't fall over, so she swung the bat and connected.

Whack.

The big canine slumped to the floor atop the wererat.

Leaning against her bat, she sighed. Two bodies to get rid of. So much for getting any more sleep tonight.

Before she could grab a rope for hauling, a throat cleared itself in her doorway.

"Sorry to bother, but did you just kill Orion?"

She glanced to see a beautiful man standing there. Ebony-skinned but with light eyes, dressed in loose khakis and a long-sleeve Henley.

"Orion?" She glanced down. "I assume you mean the dog?" Because she couldn't imagine anyone keeping the wererat as a pet. "He's not dead. Just sleeping very soundly." And would have slept forever if she'd dumped him under a nearby bridge. The troll under there appreciated the fresh meat and got rid of the evidence. She'd long ago learned the Cryptid Authority was more headache than help when it came to these kinds of random attacks.

"I told him to not rush in," the beautiful man said with a sigh and shake of his head.

"In your dog's defense, he thought I was in danger. Unfortunately for him, I wasn't sure if he'd attack me next."

The reply led to the man eyeing her taser and bat before giving her a faint smile. "It would seem you had things well in hand. Do attacks of this type happen often?"

Given she didn't know him and, again, didn't want to deal with authorities, she shook her head. "Guess the rat smelled my dinner and wanted to come in for a bite."

The man glanced at her tiny kitchen area with a frown. "I doubt it came for the salad."

How had he known? She pursed her lips. "I think you should take your dog and leave."

"I'm sorry. This must be rather disturbing. Here I am, a strange fellow on your doorstep in the middle of the night. I'm Ambrose." He held out his hand as if he expected her to shake it.

She raised her taser and said, "I'm tired and would like to go back to bed."

"Of course. If you'll give me a moment to gather my friend." She took a step back as he entered her place, but rather than approach her, he knelt by the big dog and muttered, "Idiot." He scooped the beast with little effort but then eyed the wererat still lying there.

"If you give me a moment, I'll remove this for you as well."

"No need. I can handle it."

"I'm sure you can," he murmured. "But allow me."

The man dumped the dog in the tiny outdoor landing and immediately returned to grab the wererat, slinging it over a shoulder. He stared at her, rather intently, before saying, "Sorry to have disturbed you.

Be sure to lock up." He then closed the door. She remained staring at it for a moment before engaging the locks.

What a weird night. And forget sleep.

The coffee went on early, and despite her vow to reduce her sugar intake, she made herself a batch of whipped cream to go with her strawberries for breakfast.

In retrospect, it occurred to her to wonder if the man would turn her into the authorities for harming the wererat—not that much would happen. They were considered pests, with very little cognitive thought in their tiny brains, and the minute one attacked they became fair game. That said, the paperwork could be copious, and she had better things to do.

Of interest? How the beautiful man didn't seem shocked by her actions. Even volunteered to help. He must have been walking his dog when it smelled the rat and instinct kicked in. Although who the heck walked their pet at such an ungodly hour?

Not her problem. At least he'd been polite and saved her from lugging the wererat in her large duffel that she kept for such occasions. Third home invasion this month and seventh this year.

As to why it kept happening? She hadn't the slightest clue, but it might be time to move to a more secure building—if she could afford it.

Rental prices had been skyrocketing since Covid and her current place wasn't too bad. The landlord liked her and the fact she always paid on time and that she didn't cause trouble. Moving would mean cutting back on her reading and the fund she'd been growing so she could go on a cruise.

She eyed Fudge and Smudge napping once more. "I'm going to shower. Keep an eye on the place, would you?"

Neither moved, but their tails swished. She'd bring them home something fresh for dinner; they'd earned it. Maybe she'd pick up a bone too, just in case she ran into the beautiful man and his dog again.

Then again, it might be best if they never crossed paths because Adeline tended to be bad luck to those around her. And it would be a shame if he accidentally died.

CHAPTER 3

A BEMUSED AMBROSE KNELT BESIDE AN UNCONSCIOUS ORION and poked him with a finger.

"Wake up, dumbass." He'd warned his friend to not rush in. Ambrose had wanted to observe what the wererat wanted. Yes, clearly it wanted inside Adeline's apartment; however, he couldn't help but wonder why.

Wererats weren't confrontational. Not usually. They also didn't break into places with people. They were scavengers of opportunity, enjoying freshly filled dumpsters, open windows of empty buildings, items dropped in passing. So to see one using its claws to pick a lock to get inside someone's home? Very strange.

But did Orion listen to Ambrose's caution? Nope, he went full-on furry hound and rushed in, got clocked, and now lay still in dog form on the stoop by the woman's door. Ambrose still had the wererat hefted atop his shoulder. It appeared to have a broken neck but remained alive. Good because he had questions.

Ambrose offered up a quick and silent prayer. *Hekate, sorry to bother, but it appears my companion is in need of healing.* Warmth filled him as she chose to reply.

Done.

Heat spread from his poking finger to Orion, who suddenly shuddered before his shaggy head rose and he snarled.

"Quiet," Ambrose hushed. "Let's get out of here before we draw attention." The basement apartment had a door more or less on the street, tucked under a stoop, so fairly secluded from passing foot traffic—not that there was any this time of night. But still, better to not take chances.

With the wererat firmly on his shoulder, Ambrose led them out of that cramped stairwell entrance and across the street to the SUV they'd rented. He dumped the body in the back before opening the passenger door for Orion to leap in. He took the wheel and pulled away from the curb as his friend shifted back to his human form.

A naked and grumpy-looking Orion grumbled, "She tasered me and then whacked me with a bat!"

"I told you not to rush in."

"The wererat was attacking her."

"From the looks of it, she was prepared to handle it, and you got in the way."

Orion, head stuck in a shirt as he struggled for the

sleeves, snapped, "Excuse me for trotting in for the rescue."

"Again, seems like she didn't need rescuing, or do you know many women who greet intruders with a taser and a bat?"

Orion's head popped through the fabric as he grudgingly admitted, "She's got a pretty good swing."

"She also didn't seem all that surprised," Ambrose noted. Most humans would have panicked. Yet she'd remained calm and collected, also cautious. She'd not once let her gaze stray from him.

"Probably gets home-invaded on a regular basis given her location. Why not opt for somewhere more secure?"

"I would imagine the price of rent has much to do with it." Not something Orion thought of much since Hekate provided the funds for their day-to-day expenses.

Orion shimmied into his pants, the space in the front seat making it challenging, but shifters were used to dressing in odd and tight places. They had to learn since humans had a thing about nudity in public. When done, Orion glanced behind at the cargo area.

"Where are we dumping the body? You should find somewhere close since we really should get back to her."

"First, we're going to question the rat."

"Dabbling in necromancy now, are we?" Orion stated with a smirk.

"It's not dead."

"Yeah, it is. I snapped its neck."

"But it's still breathing," Ambrose pointed out.

"Fuck off. Seriously?" Orion full-on turned in his seat. "Shit. Not sure what you think you'll get out of it, though. Wererats aren't known for their conversation skills." Unlike some shifters, the rats tended to be more like their animal counterparts.

"I want to know why it chose her," Ambrose stated, pulling into a parking lot of a business that had been boarded over. He tucked them behind the building out of sight before exiting the SUV.

Orion followed. "What makes you think it wasn't just a crime of opportunity?"

"Rats don't usually pick locks, and while they scavenge, they aren't burglars."

"Maybe this one got tired of garbage-can diving."

Ambrose shot him a look.

"What? It's possible this one craved fresher food."

"And so a carnivore went after a woman who is vegetarian."

Orion pursed his lips. "Maybe it wanted her cats. She's got two of them inside that tiny place."

"I think you should lie down. That blow to the head obviously addled what few wits you still own."

"Ha. Ha," Orion muttered. "I still can't believe she hit me."

"She hit a giant dog in her apartment," Ambrose corrected. "Not sure what you expected."

"Belly rub of thanks, for starters."

Ambrose didn't reply as he opened the trunk and heaved out the wererat with its floppy head.

He set it on the ground and crouched. *Hekate,* he called her with his mind. *If you don't mind, a little healing magic. I want to interrogate this creature and find out why it broke into the apartment owned by Adeline.*

I can't fix it. Her short reply.

His brow creased. *I know it's not an ally, but I really want to ask it a few questions before sending it on its way.*

Can't heal the dead.

He rocked back on his heels, mostly because, despite what his goddess claimed, he could see the chest still rising and falling.

Um, it's not dead, goddess. Just tasered and neck snapped.

The flesh might still appear alive, but its soul is long gone.

Well, that was unexpected. *I thought souls only left a body after death.*

That is the usual order of things. This is unnatural. His goddess didn't sound impressed.

Do you know why it was after Adeline? he asked.

Rather than reply to his question, she stated, *This isn't the first time she's dealt with such a threat.*

He'd already figured that out, given the way she'd handled the situation. *Why would a soulless wererat attack her?*

Because she is special.

Special how?

You will soon find out.

And with that final statement, the goddess was gone. The warmth that filled him when they talked quickly evaporated as the chill of night enveloped him.

"So Hekate says she can't heal the wererat because—"

"It's missing a soul," Orion interjected. "I heard, and gotta say, that's fucked up. So is it like a zombie?" Orion poked the wererat with a finger. "I thought the undead were all like rotted and stuff. Not to mention, stupid. This one opened a locked door."

"I don't know. Necromancy isn't common enough for there to be many studies."

"Was it after her brains?" Orion's eyes widened.

"Who knows," Ambrose muttered. He eyed the wererat and thus caught the flutter of its lashes.

The eyes opened, red irises kind of evil-looking, in his opinion. It hissed and snapped its teeth but couldn't lift its head or flail its arms.

Orion didn't sense any intelligence in the creature but still found himself questioning it. "Who are you? Why were you after the woman?"

Grawr. Hisssh. Blerga.

"I think it wants to eat your brains," Orion confided.

"At least I have some," his snide reply.

"Not my fault I'm extra developed below the belt instead," Orion punched back.

Ambrose snorted. "Yeah, it makes you extra stupid when aroused."

"Ouch!"

The wererat stopped snapping to eye them.

"Is it me, or is it listening?" Ambrose asked, cocking his head.

"I thought it was dead."

"Soulless. Which I'm not sure is the same thing." He'd have to brush up on his undead knowledge.

"If it's already dead, then how do we kill it? Because I assume we're not just leaving it here like this."

"Decapitation followed by fire is the usual modus operandi with zombies."

"I didn't bring a sword, did you?" Orion stated.

"No." In their line of work, usually being hounds with a bit of their goddess' magic proved to be enough.

"Chewing through its neck, then?"

Ambrose grimaced. "Also no."

"I'm open to suggestions."

"Maybe we should place an anonymous call to the CA?" The CA standing for Cryptid Authority, those who handled non-human crimes.

"What if they trace the wererat back to Adeline?"

"I don't see how they would." Ambrose leaned in for a sniff, ignoring the stench of whatever garbage pile the wererat crawled out of to see if the woman's tantalizing scent lingered. It didn't.

"It's got nothing identifying on it," Orion remarked, studying the body. It wore no clothing, just ratty fur.

"So, we're agreed? Let the CA handle the body?"

"Yeah. We can give them a shout on our way back

to watch Adeline," Orion stated as he headed for their ride.

"Already on a first-name basis?" Ambrose followed, hands shoved in his pockets.

"Well, you know, she did make me a sandwich," Orion boasted.

Ambrose rolled his eyes. "She made me one too. And?"

"You know they say the way to a man's heart is his stomach."

"Since when do you want your heart involved?"

Orion's step hitched before he offered a nonchalant. "Always a first time."

The unexpected reply almost made Ambrose fall over. "You like her?"

"She's interesting."

"You barely know her."

"And? Isn't that how the whole relationship thing starts?"

"I can't believe you just used the R word."

"I'm not getting any younger," Orion pointed out.

"Neither am I, courtesy of our goddess. But she's human."

"Who says Hekate doesn't want another scion?"

"Going to dump me?" Ambrose tried to sound light, but inside a knot formed. Didn't matter that he and Orion were complete opposites, they'd been friends for so long the thought of splitting hurt and panicked. What would he do without Orion?

"Fuck splitting up. You're my bro," Orion reassured

as he buckled up. "Who says we can't become a threesome?"

For a second, Ambrose misunderstood. "Dude, I like you and all, but I am not interested in sex with you."

"Not that kind of threesome," Orion laughed. "Although it should be noted they can be fun."

"If you're into dick, which I'm not." Some might call him close-minded for it, but Ambrose only ever found himself attracted to women.

"For your information, the swords don't need to cross in a menage."

"Don't see how you could avoid it," Ambrose stated, even as he couldn't believe they were having this conversation.

"Because you can make it all about the woman. Her pleasure. Her needs."

"One hole," his crude reply.

"Only if you lack imagination."

"Enough of this. We are not having a threesome with Adeline or anyone. I'll get my own girlfriend, thank you very much."

"Spoilsport."

Was he? They returned to Adeline's place in time to see her exiting at an ungodly early to head to work. Seeing her made his heart race. It wasn't just Orion intrigued by the woman at the midst of their mission.

One brief conversation, one sniff, and Ambrose hated to admit he might be smitten too. The sandwich helped.

However, he wouldn't act on it. Not just because Orion kind of claimed her first. While he wanted to find love, Ambrose remained aware that he wasn't an ordinary guy. He worked for a goddess. A human wouldn't understand his first duty would be to Hekate. A human would probably have a problem with the fact he could shift shapes and travel where his goddess commanded.

Or was he projecting the conventions of the time he was raised in on the modern day? Magic had become a mainstream part of life, the witch and werewolf hunts abolished, but that didn't mean everyone accepted the cryptids living amongst humans.

"Why are you looking more serious than usual?" Orion asked.

"Just thinking of the rat and why it was there."

"Maybe it wanted her cats."

"Possible. But again, why break into a tiny apartment smelling of fruits and vegetables when the alley dumpster had plenty of meat scraps? Speaking of the rat, guess we should call the CA and report it."

"No need. I filled in their anonymous tip page on the website." Orion held up his phone.

"Good."

"I'll check in later with a friend to see what they can tell us about the rat. Think they'll cremate it once they realize it's a zombie?"

"More likely they'll want to study it."

"Speaking of study, I'm going to watch the inside

of my eyelids. Want to look my best for when I go see Adeline."

"Wait, why are you going to see her?" Ambrose asked.

"She makes an awesome sandwich."

She also had an awesome ass.

Ambrose parked a few stores down only moments before she passed with a brisk stride. He slumped down as she came even with the SUV but kept an eye as she paused to unlock the store door.

When she went inside, he found himself fidgeting, not liking her being out of sight. Never mind the fact they'd placed a camera by the rear entrance that would notify him if anyone entered the alley.

Ambrose wanted another face-to-face meeting. Wanted to sniff the air she perfumed. Stare at her beautiful features. Have those tightly gripping hands—

Whoa.

He just about slapped himself for even going there. Being a perv was Orion's thing. Ambrose treated the opposite sex with respect.

But for some reason, he found it hard today.

So very, very *hard*.

CHAPTER 4

ADELINE WALKED QUICKLY TO WORK, ONE HAND IN HER pocket on the taser she'd chosen to bring along. Usually, the weird attacks were few and far between, and almost never on the street. The one time it had happened in the wee hours of the morning, a bird-faced fellow had lunged out of an alley, grabbing for her. Luckily a bystander handled the altercation, putting the attacker in a headlock while she'd fled.

While she didn't expect any trouble, she wouldn't deny the giant dog and his owner left her on edge. Yes, the man was gorgeous, and seemed rather polite, but then again, so did some mass murderers. Better safe than sorry.

She walked by an SUV, its tinted windows too dark to see within, and yet her skin prickled as if she were being watched. Not really unusual. A lone woman out this time of morning was bound to be stared at. Before dawn wasn't exactly her idea of a good start to the day. However, sitting around her apartment didn't appeal either.

She entered the shop, the little bell dinging in warning. The night crew, a bunch of elves, the tiny kind most often associated with the North Pole, paused in their restocking of the counter.

"Morning, mistress," Keeble chirped. He was the one in charge of the crew. "You're early today. Allow me just a moment to brew your tea."

Although she preferred coffee, she always made the exception for Keeble's morning tea. He'd insisted on serving her the herbal concoction since her first day on the job. Not wanting to insult their culture, she'd thanked him and drank it, and continued to drink it every day thereafter. Over time she'd grown so used to it that she even had a cup on her days off, courtesy of Keeble, who gave her a box of tea bags that couldn't be bought in stores. She figured it must have been some North Pole recipe that he'd brought to Montreal with him.

He and a dozen other elves spent the night cleaning the shop before prepping for the next day. Cooking meat, baking bread. Never mind the fact they had few clients. The leftovers were always cleared out each night to make way for fresh.

At times she wondered how the owner, whom she'd never actually met, stayed in business. Most likely the shop acted as a money-laundering front. But so long as she wasn't involved in any shady business, then she'd take the steady paycheck and easy hours. The lack of foot traffic meant she could indulge in some of her hobbies.

Right now, she was rereading *The Wheel of Time* by Robert Jordan. Great big thick books full of magic and fantasy. At times she wished she could be as gifted or special as the heroines. Alas, she'd only ever be Adeline Gagnon, one hundred percent human, whose only claim to fame was making it out of the foster system without resorting to drugs or crime.

Used to be a time when she wondered about her parents. Her file didn't have much. Mom dead when she was just a toddler. The autopsy report, which she'd managed to get a hold of, claimed she died of fright, most likely cause being a bogeyman. Apparently, they couldn't find any family members to take her in, and the name of her dad remained blank on her birth certificate. With no family options, she went into the system and got shuffled around.

A lot.

See, Adeline from a young age appeared to be plagued by bad luck. One foster mother even called it a curse. As if she could be blamed for the accidents that killed some of those caring for her. Like Mr. Goram, the foster dad who liked to watch her bathe and came into her room late at night breathing heavily. He'd tried to touch her once in the tub, and Adeline screamed, which led to him being startled, falling backward, and slamming his head on the toilet. He would have survived had his hand not been in the bowl touching water when his razor, still plugged in, fell off a shelf and electrocuted him.

There was Mrs. Hillary, who decided Adeline needed constant correction, but the day she took the belt to Adeline, it somehow became tangled in a ceiling fan and wrapped around her neck.

At the age of twelve, she did end up with a nice older couple who appreciated the fact she cleaned up after herself and never got into trouble. She never had any problems with them and stayed there until graduation. Mr. and Mrs. Grimmer passed away while she was at college, and after that, she remained pretty much a loner.

She did date. Her longest relationship lasted three years until she caught Joe in bed with a coworker. Poor Joe ended up dying within the hour, as the lube he'd been using contained an ingredient that triggered a fatal allergic reaction.

Most guys she met didn't make it past a few months. According to them, she was boring. And? She had no problem with that. She liked her life. Simple. Satisfying. Now, if only the night visits by various cryptids would stop. They'd begun a few years ago. She'd heard a scratching at her door and opened it to find a goblin on her step. Considered pests, but harmless.

It launched itself at her, and she'd instinctively slapped it aside. When it came at her a second time, she'd grabbed the nearest thing, which happened to be an umbrella, and swung. The makeshift bat whacked the goblin and sent it airborne, shattering her window.

The resulting investigation by the Cryptid Authority came back claiming it must have been rabid and she wasn't charged with murder. She should hope not—it had attacked her! The law stated if a cryptid acted in a way that made a human fear for their life, they could use deadly force. Not to mention, it hadn't died. After its fall out of the window of her previous apartment, she'd seen it twitching on the pavement, trying to crawl away.

The goblin was only the start.

Since then she'd dealt with a few wererats, more goblins, a fairy, and more recently a leprechaun, which really surprised since she had no gold or rainbows.

At times she wondered why they seemed so attracted to her. Or her apartments, at least. She'd moved after the first goblin incident—because the landlord evicted her, claiming she was up to no good. She'd lucked out finding her basement apartment with its cheap rent, but given the three attacks this month alone, it might be time to think about moving before something much meaner tried to break in. She had no training for taking out bigger monsters, nor did she have any interest. Perhaps she needed a new brand of soap? Did they sell a repellent that actually worked, because, thus far, everything she'd tried failed.

The shop opened early despite the fact they rarely

had clients before lunch. She had a nice coffee, enjoyed her vegan muffin, and read a few chapters but remembered little of it.

A bit after ten, the bell rang, and she glanced up to see the handsome man from the day before. Blond, very good-looking, with a thousand-watt smile. On his previous visit he'd flirted with her, or attempted to, but she hadn't responded. She couldn't afford to get fired for acting inappropriately with a client. But he sure did tempt...

"Hello, sir. What can I get you?"

"How about a knife to stab myself for calling me sir," he grimaced, and it only made him cuter.

"Apologies, young lad." She kept a straight face, and he laughed.

"How about calling me by name? Orion," he offered with a smile.

She blurted out, "You have the same name as a dog."

He blinked.

She quickly stammered, "Sorry. I recently met someone with a dog by that name."

"Don't apologize. I love canines, and I am honored to share a distinguished name with a princely hound."

She could have screwed with him and stated it had been a mangy mutt, but honestly, the dog had been sleek and handsome.

"What would you like today?" she asked.

"I see your special is honey garlic beef strips with provolone on a toasted kaiser."

"Is it?" She glanced behind her. She didn't create the menus, just served whatever the elves prepped. "Would you like that?"

"Yes, as well as the same ham sandwich from before for my friend."

"He's not a guy who likes change," she commented, turning to grab the right breads.

"He's very particular and set in his ways. Unlike me. I love new things." He leaned on her counter with a winsome smile, which, more than likely, got him freebies from all kinds of people. Not her. Adeline took her job seriously.

"Would you like to add veggies? It will be extra," she added.

"How about extra meat instead?"

"Also an upcharge."

"Of course, there is," he muttered with a head shake. "Have to say your prices are a little up there compared to most."

"Says the guy who's back for a second run." The flippant comment escaped her, but he didn't take offense.

His lips quirked. "It was a damned good sandwich."

"Hence you got what you paid for."

"Your store doesn't seem too busy," he noted, looking around.

"Quality over quantity is the owner's motto." Her usual reply when people felt a need to comment.

"Does the owner ever come into the shop?"

"Nope." She only ever spoke to Mr. Charyx via text or email. For her interview, he'd sent her a questionnaire. She'd thought it might be a scam until the offer of employment arrived, along with a key to the store.

"Are you here alone? And before you think I'm being creepy, I'm just wondering who does all the cooking and cleaning."

"We have a night staff to handle food prep and sanitation." She finished wrapping the sandwiches and rang his purchase through at the register.

He handed over several bills and murmured, "Keep the change."

"Thanks."

He didn't leave immediately.

"Was there something else?" she asked.

"Would you like to go for a coffee or dinner sometime?"

She blinked in surprise. She almost sounded shy. "Sorry, but I don't date customers."

"What if I promised to never buy another sandwich?"

His earnest question almost made her smile and agree. "Sorry, but I still have to say no. Enjoy your lunch."

"I doubt it, as it will be too salty."

She frowned. "I didn't put any salt on your meat."

"From my tears of disappointment."

That drew a snort. "I'm sure you'll survive."

"Barely." He clutched his chest.

"Goodbye, Orion."

"Goodbye, Adeline."

Only as he walked out the door did she realize, *I never told him my name.*

CHAPTER 5

SHIT. ORION KNEW HE'D FLUBBED THE MOMENT HE SAID HER name. Would she notice? Maybe she'd assume she'd told him already.

Fuck.

As he climbed into the SUV, a napping Ambrose opened an eye and muttered, "What did you do now?"

"What makes you think I did anything?" Orion huffed, handing over a sandwich.

"I've known you too long. I know that face, the one that screams, 'I messed up.'"

Orion sighed. "I used her name."

"Let me guess. She never introduced herself."

"No, but she did tell me when I told her mine that she knew a dog by the same name." He glared at his friend.

"When I first went to your rescue, I thought she'd killed you and might have mentioned it."

"Great, when she thinks of the name Orion, she's going to associate it with a dog."

"You are one, both figuratively and literally," Ambrose pointed out.

"Not helping," he grumbled, taking a bite from his epic sandwich. He spent a few minutes groaning through each savory bite before leaning back with a sigh. "What's on the agenda for today?"

"Watching our target."

"Yeah, we both know we're wasting our time parked on the street."

"What are you suggesting?"

"One of us should be checking out her apartment."

"Checking it for what exactly?" Ambrose asked with a furrowed brow.

"Threats. Other points of egress. Perhaps a reason why our goddess and a soulless wererat are so interested in her.

"Actually, not a bad idea. Go ahead."

"Me? Why not you?"

"Because you've already been inside her shop today. Meaning, if she spots you out here, then she might have questions."

"She might have some if she sees you as well, seeing as how you met last night."

"I won't be seen," Ambrose confidently declared. "Although I will be checking the alley."

"For what? We have cameras watching the rear door into the shop." Not actually their camera. They'd hacked into the security ones already available.

"I noticed an interesting lack of the usuals in the alley." Before Orion could ask, Ambrose listed them. "No goblins, despite the two dumpsters with food scraps." Goblins being nature's solution to food waste recycling. "There's also been no hint of any cryptids at all in the space."

"We've only been watching a week."

"Watching an alley with food waste that connects to a major thoroughfare and has not one but two sewer grates. It should be a hotspot."

Orion pondered the very valid point. "Maybe I should take the alley. I've got a keener nose."

"Which will be perfect for her apartment. Me, I have this." Ambrose held up a bag of herbs.

"Smells nasty." Orion wrinkled his nose.

"It's charmed to glow around stationary spells and give me an idea what kind it is. Red for danger, AKA a trap. Green for monitoring of the area. Yellow for concealment. And blue for repelling."

"You never told me you suspected her alley was hexed!"

Ambrose shrugged. "Seemed kind of obvious after a few days, so I had Mindy over in Nexus whip me up something to use."

"You could have mentioned it," Orion grumbled.

"I am."

"Ass."

Ambrose grinned. "You're just peeved I thought of it."

A reply didn't happen because his phone rang. He

glanced at the number. "It's my contact at the Montreal CA." He answered. "Hey, Carly."

Rather than greet him, she whispered, "What the heck are you involved in?"

"What do you mean?" he replied cautiously.

"That wererat we picked up? The one you wanted me to look into?"

"Yeah. What about it?"

"It's been confiscated. And by confiscated, I mean dudes in dark suits and glasses showed up, seized the rat, decontaminated the cells, took all the paper trail to it, deleted the request for it to be picked up, and now people are being called in one by one to the boss's office."

"Who are the suits?" he asked.

"Dunno, but the boss isn't arguing with them."

"Sounds like a coverup of some sort," Orion mused aloud.

"Which is why I asked what you're involved in."

"Any idea what people are being told in your boss's office?"

"I'm about to find out; it's my turn. Hold on. I'm going to slip you into my pocket so you can have a listen." Rustling ensued as Carly tucked him away, muffled but he could still make out noise, such as the voice of the woman saying, "Agent Mathews?"

"Yes, that's me."

"Please have a seat."

"Okay. What's this about? What's going on?"

"Please look at this medallion."

"Isn't that a..." Carly trailed off, and a hum had Orion holding the phone away from his ear. When the noise ended, the same woman said, "Thank you, Agent Mathews, you may return to work."

Orion listened as Carly exited, the door shutting with a firm click. She strode back to her desk, and he heard a creak as she sat then a curse. "Why is my phone in my pocket?"

He held the phone away again, as the noise of her removing it proved annoying to his ears. Once it stopped, he whispered, "Carly?"

"Hello?" She spoke tentatively. "Who is this?"

"Orion," he answered with a frown.

"Did I butt-dial you?"

"No, you called me, remember? To talk about the wererat and the suits?"

"What rat? What suits? Are you drunk already?"

Orion's mouth rounded, and he glanced at Ambrose, who pursed his lips and mouthed, *Hang up.*

Orion cleared his throat. "Ha, just messing with you. Was going to say we should meet up for a drink while I'm in town."

"Sure, but I'll have to bring my husband. He got insanely jealous the last time we had a coffee together."

"Sounds good. I'll text soon." Orion hung up and glanced at Ambrose. "They whammied Carly."

"And everyone else in that office," Ambrose's grim reply.

"Over a wererat?" Orion couldn't hold back an incredulous note.

"Not just a wererat, one without a soul. Meaning there's something big afoot, with enough clout behind it to wipe all records, even memories, of the incident."

Left unsaid—somehow Adeline was involved.

CHAPTER 6

Adeline found herself unable to concentrate on her book. Blame the fact she'd looked out the front window and happened to see a man with dark skin exiting the SUV that had been parked across the street for the past week. A man who looked an awful lot like Ambrose, the guy she'd met very early this morning.

As the SUV drove off, the man crossed the street. She couldn't see where he went, though, without stepping outside.

She set her book aside and stood to stretch. Maybe some air would do her good. She headed for the front door and was about to open it when an altercation broke out. Two cars trying to park in one spot. It led to them both blocking the road to get out and yell at each other.

Rather than get drawn into the drama, she exited out the back door into the alley, only to startle at the sight of the gorgeous man from the previous night standing there holding up a glowing blue bag.

He froze, arm upraised at the sight of her.

"What are you doing?" she asked.

"Nothing."

She arched a brow. "Doesn't look like nothing."

Ambrose lowered his arm and cleared his throat. "I meant I'm not doing anything yet. This is simply an inspection."

"Inspection for what? Is there a problem?" She wasn't aware of any health violations or issues. Unlike other places in the city, the alley behind the shop remained well-kept and problem-free.

"No problem. Just routine checking."

Something about his actions and claim sounded off. "Ordered by who?" She crossed her arms and fixed him with a stare.

"Uh…"

Her gaze narrowed. "Are you stalking me?"

"Wh-what? No!" he stammered.

"Yet here you are, twice in one day. Seems like more than a coincidence."

"I assure you, ma'am, I mean you no harm."

She almost grimaced at his use of ma'am. Way to make her feel old. "Says the guy who was walking his dog at an ungodly hour, who didn't blink at the unconscious wererat in my place, and who is now suspiciously waving around a magic bag in the alley by my work."

"You needn't worry. I work for the CA," he blurted out. "Special operations."

"In that case, you'll have no problem showing me your badge."

"I'm afraid I left it in my vehicle."

"Of course, you did," her dry reply.

"I could run back and grab it," he offered.

"Don't bother. Your partner left with the SUV. Convenient."

"I swear I mean you no harm, ma'am."

"My name is Adeline." Why she told him she couldn't have said. "And I want to know what you're looking for."

He glanced at the bag dangling from his hand and sighed. "I'm looking to see if there are spells in the alley."

While her first impulse would be to deny any, she had to wonder, given the blue glow of his sack. "What kind of spells?"

"That's what this is supposed to tell me." He shook it. "It is supposed to detect the genre of spell and emit a color accordingly."

"But doesn't disarm them?"

He shook his head.

"Why would anyone spell this alley, not to mention, why send anyone to check?"

"I'm afraid I am not at liberty to discuss those matters," his stiff reply.

"Well then, in that case, don't let me keep you. Inspect away." She waved at him, and he stared at her for a second before abruptly pivoting and crossing the alley to the other building with the door to the dry cleaners. He held up the bag, which continued to glow blue.

Adeline remained propped in the open door to listen for a customer while watching Ambrose walk the length of the alley and back. His bag remained alight right up to the entrance. When he walked back, she had to ask, "So, what have you concluded?"

"Someone placed a hex on your alley."

"What kind of hex?"

"The kind to repel cryptids. I'm going to guess you never see goblins around? Or any other nonhuman species?"

Her lips pursed as she replied slowly, "You know what, I haven't, not in the alley at least. The elves who work overnight come up through the basement. Never occurred to me that someone might have done something on purpose. Isn't it illegal?" She could have sworn they'd made a law declaring repelling spells on what were considered public venues illegal. Personal homes and businesses, though, could do so as long as the repelling caused no harm.

"Yes. But it's not uncommon for businesses to try and protect themselves."

"I wonder if I should get one for my place." It might help with her home invasion problem but would put a serious dent in her savings.

"That's an excellent idea. I know a few witches who could help with it."

"So are you going to have the spell removed?" she asked.

"Not yet. I want to see if I can figure out who placed it and why."

"Wasn't me." She held up her hands. "One hundred percent human and too broke to even think of doing it for an alley I rarely visit."

"What of the owner?"

"Mr. Charyx? He never comes by."

"Do you have contact info for your employer?"

"Only if you're showing me a badge. But if you give me your phone number or email, I can pass a message along."

"No need. I'll find the information myself."

If he truly did work for the CA, then he'd have no problem.

"You don't have your dog today," she remarked.

"Orion is off doing his own thing." He waved a hand. "He can be a tad independent."

"Ironically enough I had a client this morning named Orion."

"I know. He's my partner."

She stared at him before slowly saying, "You named your dog after your partner?"

Ambrose cracked a smile. "Actually, they're one and the same. In the spirit of being transparent, we're both shifters."

The news dropped her jaw. "Wait, you mean I knocked out your partner last night?"

"Yeah. Insulted him too, seeing as how he rushed

in to be the hero, only to get taken out. Thanks. It was kind of awesome." The smile he offered just about melted her into a puddle of goo.

"Glad to help?" Her reply lilted, and she found herself grinning. "So you're the guy who's no pickles, no lettuce, add bacon."

"Yeah. I'm a creature of habit."

"Nothing wrong with knowing what you like."

She might have made more small talk, but the bell to the store actually jingled. A customer? Seriously. And here she'd been enjoying chatting with the handsome CA agent. "Guess I'd better go do my job."

"It was nice speaking with you," he stated. "Maybe we'll have a chance to do so again."

"I'd like that." Unlike his partner, Ambrose didn't flirt outrageously.

Did she think it would go anywhere?

Most likely not, but she went back inside smiling.

CHAPTER 7

Orion scowled. His mission to inspect Adeline's apartment turned out to be a disaster. Getting the door unlocked, easy enough, but once inside, he'd been confronted by her two cats. They currently had him penned in the bathroom, which was where he called Ambrose from.

"Hey, did you find something?" his friend asked.

"No, because I'm stuck in the bathroom."

"Why would you try and climb through that tiny window?" Ambrose exclaimed.

"I didn't. I came through the front door, only her cats lost their shit."

"And?"

"And they chased me into the bathroom and won't let me out."

Ambrose laughed. Really long and hard, leading Orion to tightly snap, "Not funny. How am I supposed to check her apartment for clues, not to mention get out, before she gets home?"

"I don't get it. You're usually so good with pussies," Ambrose taunted.

"Have you seen the size of them? I mean I smelled them last night, but I don't remember seeing the beasts."

"You were kind of busy. Since when you are afraid of a ten-to-fifteen-pound cat?"

"Try cougar sized."

"Er, what?" Ambrose huffed in surprise.

"You'll see when you get here. Hurry."

"Hurry how? You took the SUV."

"So, run. It's not that far."

"I am not sprinting and getting all sweaty."

"It's kind of urgent," Orion muttered through gritted teeth.

"Not really. You're in the bathroom, meaning you're safe for the moment."

Safe, yes. However, being trapped irked. "What am I supposed to do while I wait?"

"Piss on something. You love marking your territory."

He did; however, Orion usually did that outside. "Move your ass," he grumbled before hanging up. He planted his hands on his hips and glared at the bathroom door. When he'd first walked in after picking the lock—which really could have used a more intricate mechanism and a protection spell—he'd been confronted by two small kitties with hackles raised, emitting low growls. He'd paid them no mind as he stepped past until he heard their growls deepen. A glance over his shoulder showed the normal-sized pussies had expanded to jungle-cat-sized.

Now, he could have shifted and taken them on, but he hesitated for a few reasons. One, it would draw attention. Two, a fight would have damaged Adeline's apartment, and three, these were her pets. He doubted she'd take kindly to him harming them.

He had to wonder how much the spell cost to have her felines able to expand their girth to act as guard dogs. Probably a lot more than a real dog would cost.

I'll never live this down. In Ambrose's defense, if the roles were reversed, Orion would be merciless with his teasing as well.

It took forever for Ambrose to make the walk from the sandwich shop, and Orion only knew he'd arrived because he heard him exclaim, "Nice kitties. Look what I brought."

Orion dared to open the door for a peek and saw Ambrose unwrapping some butcher paper to reveal fat fish. A pair, meaning each cat grabbed one and slunk off, their massive bodies shrinking as they strode. There was something ironic about seeing them go from having a snack-sized fish in their mouth to one almost as big as them when they returned to their original size.

"You can come out now," Ambrose announced. "I have saved you from the vicious kitties."

"Fuck off," Orion muttered. "I didn't want to hurt them."

"I should hope not, since they were just doing their job. While I noticed them this morning during the wererat altercation, I never suspected they were hallowed."

"You mean magicked," Orion corrected.

Ambrose shook his head. "Take a proper sniff. No magic. They appear to be god-blessed, just like us."

"Why would a human have divinely altered cats?"

The query led to Ambrose shrugging. "I imagine for the same reason the entire alley behind her shop has a cryptid repellent. A strong hex. Very unpleasant. Even I felt it." While Orion and Ambrose could shift, their gift wasn't naturally born but one given to them by the Goddess Hekate. Some called them scions. God-blessed was another word. Even the term disciples applied, depending on the god.

"We should get the search done before the beasts finish their bribe and come after us again," Orion noted, keeping his eye on the cats. They appeared normal as they munched, nothing like the snarling creatures that tried to attack.

"It shouldn't take long. This place is tiny," Ambrose remarked.

Indeed, they usually stayed in larger hotel rooms. Glancing around, Orion almost shuddered. He couldn't imagine living in what amounted to not more than a cave. Little daylight came through the window.

The ceilings were barely seven feet. Might as well live in a prison.

They searched the place thoroughly, opening every cupboard and drawer, flipping cushions off the couch to see it held a bed—the scent of her rising from the sheets. Delectable. Orion couldn't help but inhale and noticed Ambrose doing the same.

They looked under furniture, tapped for hidden panels, even checked the water tank on the toilet and found nothing. A thorough sniff of the place also didn't reveal anything. No hints of magic, blood, or decay. Just a hint of mildew because of the basement aspect, fishy feline, and Adeline.

"There's nothing here," Orion declared with surprise.

Ambrose held up his spell-detecting bag, and it remained dark. "It's spell-free."

"No magic. No meat. No riches. Makes you wonder why that wererat would have targeted her place." The behavior was out of character. "We should have tried questioning it for longer," Orion grumbled.

"Pretty sure we would have never deciphered its grunts and snarks."

"No, but we could have taken him to a witch and had her do a memory spell on it. We might have seen why it targeted her place."

"You think it was intentional?" Ambrose asked.

"Yeah, but struggling to find a reason why. Unless it's about revenge. Maybe an ex-boyfriend or someone she pissed off. I mean those sandwich prices are a bit nuts."

"When I spoke to her—"

"When did you talk to her?" Orion blurted out.

"She kind of caught me in the alley when I tested for magic. We had a short chat, and while she didn't say anything, I'm getting the strong feeling this wasn't the first time this has happened."

"No, shit," Orion huffed. "I mean she confronted it and me, with a taser and a bat." He knew firsthand she could wield them proficiently. "The bigger question remains, though, why her?"

"I don't know, but I will wager that it is wrapped into the reason why our goddess sent us to watch over her."

"Speaking of watch, at least one of us should get back to her shop before it closes." Orion felt a nagging sense of unease. The babysitting job had gone from boring to intriguing and not just because of the wererat and blessed kitties. There was something about Adeline...

"We'll both go. I think her place is well guarded enough." Ambrose glanced at the cats who rested in the window, fish gone, eyes closed, tails tucked around their bodies.

"Is she guarded? They didn't do shit against the wererat."

"Maybe because they knew she could handle it?" Ambrose suggested.

"Maybe." Orion glanced at the two pussies as they

headed out the door, and one cocked open a single eye that glowed green for a second, giving a clue.

Could it be the Earth goddess that blessed them? She usually stuck to plants, but as a deity of extreme power, giving some cats the ability to bulk up wouldn't be a stretch. But why would the Earth Mother be providing Adeline protection?

And why did Hekate do the same?

What made Adeline special?

Time to do some digging to find out.

CHAPTER 8

THE CUSTOMER WHO ENTERED THE SHOP TURNED TAIL AND fled when he saw the prices. Just came in long enough to foil her chat with the handsome CA agent. Assuming he told the truth. Then again, why lie? He did fit the profile. Good looking and confident. Driving a blacked-out SUV. Doing weird shit he couldn't explain.

Like, why would the CA care about spells in the alley... unless... could it be her boss was about to go down? Adeline knew enough about business to know the shop had to be losing money hand over fist. She'd worked here eighteen years, with yearly pay raises, even a pension plan and medical insurance, all costly. Never once had Mr. Charyx complained about the lack of customers to justify her salary and benefits. It could only mean one thing.

The shop acted as a front for money laundering. If authorities were about to move in and make arrests, would anyone believe Adeline when she claimed innocence? Hopefully, they'd look at her living situation and bank account. Enough for her needs, no big extras. They'd soon realize she didn't profit off any ill-gotten gains.

An investigation would probably mean Ambrose would be back, along with his partner. Orion, the dog. Also, very good-looking and super charming—in human form.

Wait, had he flirted with her in the hopes of cozying up and pumping her for information? It would make sense, assuming the whole secret agent thing was true. Without a badge number, she couldn't exactly call to check.

When closing time arrived, she didn't have to do anything but gather her stuff and go, locking the door behind her. The overnight crew would handle everything else. As she walked, she glanced over and noticed the SUV parked in its spot. Would it trail her?

She stared forward and went a block before glancing over her shoulder to see it creeping.

Yup. Stalking. Ignore or confront?

Before she could overthink it, she crossed the road, marching for the vehicle, which pulled over and stopped by the curb. As she approached the driver side window, it rolled down, and she saw Ambrose behind the wheel with Orion in the passenger seat.

"You're following me," she stated without preamble.

"Just making sure you get home safe," Ambrose's lame excuse.

She arched a brow. "I walk this way every day and have for a long time."

"After what happened with that wererat—"

"What of it? I would have handled it if your dog partner hadn't interfered."

"Dog?" Orion piped up. "You told her?"

Ambrose glanced at his friend. "She would have figured it out sooner or later."

Actually, she probably wouldn't have, but she didn't correct him. "Why are you really following me? And don't give me some baloney about it being unsafe for me. Is this about my job?"

"I don't think so," Ambrose replied slowly.

"But I am a person of interest in whatever you're investigating," she pushed.

"Yes, but not in the way you think," Ambrose stated without clarifying.

"I know nothing, so before you drag me in for interrogation, whatever it is you're looking for, I am not involved."

"Are you sure about that?" Orion leaned over to ask.

"Pretty sure. I hate to break it to you, but I am a very boring person. I work in a dull going-nowhere job, live with two cats, and occasionally have to deal with cryptids breaking in. That's it." Too late she realized she'd let that slip.

"How often has it happened?" Ambrose asked with a serious expression.

"For a few years now." She shrugged. "I should probably change apartments again, but the rent is right and the commute easy. It seemed simpler to get a taser to handle it."

"Have you been reporting these attacks?"

If they truly were CA agents, they would already know she'd never filed any complaints after the first incident. She bit her lower lip before shaking her head. "I haven't called anyone about the break-ins, not since the first one, which turned out to be a giant headache of paperwork."

"Is it always wererats?" Orion jumped in to ask.

"Usually but not always. I've also dealt with a leprechaun, some goblins, and a fairy." The last one she'd felt bad about because she found them super cute, but when it launched itself at her, hissing, she'd whacked it with a frying pan, and well, it didn't survive.

"Did you ever notice anything strange about those you've confronted?" Ambrose had a slight crease to his brow. "Perhaps odd behavior?"

"Odder than trying to rob someone with very little?" She shrugged. "Not really. Maybe my apartment is some kind of magic hotspot. Could even be the previous tenant used to have business with them."

"Business with wererats and goblins?" Orion snorted.

"I told you I don't know why. Just gave a possibility, which, I'll admit, is probably farfetched, but at the same time, I don't understand why it keeps happening."

"Have any of them ever hurt you?" Ambrose changed the line of questioning.

"Only one came close. It broke in through my window before the landlord had the bars installed. It might have ended badly for me if I'd not grabbed a kitchen knife." Hence how she knew what a mess a bladed weapon could be. After that incident, she'd gone shopping for a bat and then later the taser.

"What about the cats?" Orion pointedly asked.

"What about them? I found them in the alley behind the shop and adopted them."

"You found them?" Ambrose sounded surprised.

"Yeah. I thought it would be nice to have them as pets, only they're a tad standoffish. But they're company, and even better, they wake me up when someone tries to come in."

"How many intruders have they handled?" Orion queried.

She snorted. "None. You have seen the size of them, right? They let me know we have company, and I take care of the rest."

"When you say, 'take care,' what exactly do you do with the intruders?"

Her lips clamped tight. Now wasn't the right time to incriminate herself by admitting she dumped them under a bridge for the troll to dispose of. "Knock them out and toss them to the road."

"Even the dead ones?"

"Who says I kill them?" she riposted. As if she'd admit to anything.

Ambrose's expression clearly said he didn't believe her, but he didn't prod. Orion did.

"You mean to tell me, after zapping their butts, they don't come back for revenge?"

"Why would they do that when there's easier pickings?" Her breezy reply. "Now, while this has been enlightening, I need to get home to feed my cats. Feel free to follow, although I should mention I've never been burglarized before midnight, so you'll be wasting your time."

"Get in and we'll give you a lift," Ambrose offered.

Get in a vehicle with two strangers, who may or may not be CA agents? Which reminded, she'd yet to see a badge. "Where's your ID?"

"What ID?" Orion repeated.

"I'm afraid I was mistaken earlier when I said I had my CA badge in the SUV. It appears I left it at the hotel." Ambrose neatly supplied.

"Of course, you did," she muttered. She turned from them and headed back across the street to resume walking home. She didn't need to turn her head to know they crept behind. It oddly reassured. She'd slightly fibbed about never having confronted anything after work because it only happened the one time. It probably helped she rarely went out at night. Her evenings were spent watching television, which did little for her social life. Then again, she didn't make friends easily. The few she'd had over the years never lasted. Not because they drifted apart or lost interest. Her friends had a tendency of dying via freak accidents.

Ever watch any of the Final Destinations with the fluke events determined to kill people? Very much like her friends. The last one, several years ago, Dolly, had died after a night out at the movies. Even worse, they'd argued about a stupid plot point. They'd split up, both pissed, but Adeline never had a chance to apologize. On the bus ride home, something in the road caused the driver to swerve, hit a curb, and tilt up on two wheels before flipping right over, crushing a guard rail, rolling down a steep incline, and landing in a stormwater catch basin. Poor Dolly drowned.

Then there was her college friend, Anita. They were actually in their room—Adeline studying, while Anita boasted about how she wasted her time because she already had the answers to the test—when a pipe in the upstairs bathroom burst. The water seeped through the ceiling into the light socket and jetted down to hit Anita in the head, electrocuting her.

There were others. A guy she was casually dating, John, got hit by not one but two buses while crossing on his light right after dumping her for refusing to have a threesome. Jane, from high school, went to prom with Adeline, and on the limo ride home, as she ranted about the fact Adeline had gotten rid of the smuggled flask, Jane got hit by lightning through the open moonroof.

She chalked up the many deaths of people close to her as being unlucky but also used it as an excuse to recluse herself. Hence why she didn't change jobs or apartments. Her job involved little interaction. Her apartment suited her need to hide away. The upstairs units, rented month to month like hers, had a high turnover rate, so she never got to know anyone, never had to see them freakily die.

Speaking of her place, she saw it up ahead. As she passed the window, she spotted her cats lying in it. She entered and stopped dead at the strong odor of fish. Odd since she'd fed them kibble in the morning.

"Hey, Smudge and Fudge." Usually they barely acknowledged her presence, but today, Fudge jumped to the floor and sauntered over to rub against her legs and utter a meow.

She blinked. "Hi, big guy. What's up? You hungry?" Neither came running as she opened the fridge. They did, however, stare intently at the bathroom door.

The food plates went on the floor and remained untouched. Odd and completely out of character for her hungry felines. Adeline stepped past them to open the washroom door, saying, "Mind if I go pee?"

They did mind, seeing as how they both flew into the room and began prowling the space, sniffing. The shower drew their avid interest, and they sat on opposite sides of the drain.

Weird, but they were cats after all. She peed, washed her hands, and left them to wait for whatever bug they thought might be down there. Basement apartments occasionally had roaches or other nasty beetle-type bugs come crawling out. Not that she'd seen any since she got her cats. So if they wanted to lie in wait for whatever skittered, have at it.

Nothing in the fridge appealed for dinner. The vegetables required work to make them edible. Given her restlessness, she opted to go out. The vegan bistro down the street did a mean deep-fried tofu and lentil salad.

When she exited her place, she half expected to see Ambrose and Orion parked nearby. They weren't, of course. Why would they be? They claimed to just want to escort her safely home. But she had her doubts. How long before they came knocking in an official capacity?

She kept a hand on the taser in her handbag, just in case. Them asking about her nocturnal visitors had roused her anxiety. They'd implied the actions of those burglar cryptids had been out of character. She wouldn't know since she hadn't interacted with many before that.

The vegan place, *Green Tongue,* had plenty of seating. They always did, which made her worried about their long-term prospects. The last three restaurants in walking distance started out busy but tapered off to the point they shut down. Perhaps they needed someone like Mr. Charyx with deep pockets to keep things afloat.

As she ate, she glanced around at the few patrons. A man with bushy sideburns seated with a woman of uncommon beauty. An older couple, both male, graying and having an intense discussion, judging by their expressions and waving hands.

A man entered, dressed in a rumpled suit, his eyes bloodshot and his skin ashen. He didn't look well, and wouldn't you know, he headed right for her table and sat down.

"I'm sorry. Can I help you?" she asked, her fork poised midair.

The man stared at her before slowly saying, "I need it."

"Need what? Are you hungry? Do you want me to buy you some food?" He might not look homeless, but poverty could hit anyone at any time.

"You have some. I can sense it. I need it."

"I'm sorry. I think you have the wrong person." Adeline glanced to the side to see if she could spot a waiter for some help.

The man lunged forward to grab her hand, his flesh clammy and cold. He gripped her tightly as he hissed, "Give it to me. I can't stand the emptiness."

She tugged, yanking her hand free before huffing, "I don't know who you are or what you want, but you're making me very uncomfortable, so if you'll excuse me..." She rose from her chair, but so did he.

"Fix me!" the man insisted.

"I'm not a doctor. Go to the hospital." She began backing away, but he kept pace. No one in the place did a thing, even as they watched—and of course one of them filmed. Damn society. No one ever wanted to get involved anymore for fear of social media backlash.

"Liar. Give it," he growled before diving at Adeline.

Before he could connect, someone stood between them, a bigger man who barked, "Keep your hands to yourself, asshole."

Orion?

Before she could blink in surprise, a hand on her arm had her whirling to see Ambrose had also entered. "Let Orion handle him. Come." He tugged.

"But my bill..." She'd only just gotten her dinner.

Ambrose dug into his pocket and tossed cash on the counter where the waiter stood watching and not interfering. "Dinner is paid. Let's get out of here."

A part of her wanted to stay and watch, but a different part wanted as far away as she could get from the misbehaving man. He obviously suffered from some kind of mental episode.

She exited with Ambrose but didn't spot the SUV. "Where are we going?"

"We'll head back to your place for the moment."

Her head swiveled to peek behind. "What of Orion? Shouldn't you help him?"

"Orion's a big boy who can handle himself."

"I don't know what's wrong with that man, though. I think he's having a manic episode. He could be armed and dangerous."

"So is Orion," Ambrose stated with a chuckle. "Trust me, he's faced worse."

As they walked, their pace brisk, she stated, "You

were following me." The only explanation for how quickly they'd intervened.

"We did."

"Why? And don't give me some lame excuse about it being a secret. I have a right to know why CA agents are spying on me."

Ambrose shoved his hands into his pockets, ducked his head, and murmured, "I'm not a CA agent."

"Aha. I knew it!" she crowed.

"I'm a scion for the Goddess Hekate."

The unexpected reply had her tripping on the sidewalk. Ambrose reached out to steady her.

"Careful there."

She tilted her chin to meet his gaze. "I don't believe you."

The corner of his mouth lifted. "I assure you, it's true."

"You don't look like a priest."

He snorted, "Because I'm not. I am a scion, what you might term her right hand on Earth, carrying out her wishes."

"Her wishes being what?"

"That varies. Sometimes we eliminate a threat. Other times she has us seeking out things. We also provide protection to people of importance."

"Which am I?"

"Person of importance."

That had her uttering a very unladylike sound. "Now I know you're lying. There's no reason for a goddess or her lackeys to be interested in me."

"And yet here we are."

"If you truly do talk to a goddess, prove it."

"If you insist." He closed his eyes, and his lips moved soundlessly. He began to glow, radiating pink.

"Cute magic trick," she stated, "but that doesn't prove anything."

"Does this?" a female voice said inside her head.

Despite not moving, and having her eyes wide open, Adeline suddenly found herself in a strange place, the floor white marble with streaks of hot pink. Matching pillars rose into clouds, but she could see no walls, just a lounging bed, the couch kind with a partial back and a single arm. A woman lay upon it, wearing a gown of filmy white, her fuchsia hair bound in intricate ringlets upon her head.

"Hello, Adeline." The woman spoke in a husky voice.

"Um, who are you? Where am I?"

"In my domain. My scion prayed to me and mentioned you sought proof of his words."

"You're the Goddess Hekate?" She couldn't help but sound skeptical.

"Yes, in a form that appeals to you visually. Not something I do often, as it feels so very confining." Hekate grimaced as she looked at herself.

"Ambrose works for you?"

"He and Orion have been serving me for quite some time."

"Why are your servants following me?"

Hekate leaned forward as if to see Adeline better. "Because you're going to need their help."

"With what?"

"That isn't quite clear yet. The future is murky around you, Adeline."

"Why would you care about my future?"

"Because you are special."

Adeline snorted. "Wrong person." The definition of bland and boring probably had her picture alongside it.

"Oh, I'm never wrong, child," Hekate purred. "And while I am not entirely sure why you're special, I do know it's important to keep you safe, hence why I've added my aid to Gaia's."

"Gaia, as in Mother Earth?" The hallucination got weirder. It should be known that, while Adeline did believe in Gods, she didn't worship any. Why would a normal human bother? She had no magic, no cryptid blood in her ancestry. She should know, since she'd had her blood tested.

"Yes, Gaia was the first to extend her protection. Subtly of course. While we are mostly prevented from direct intervention, we can skirt that restriction by providing help in the form of believers. Thus did I send you two of my most favored. You're welcome, by the way."

"I didn't ask for your disciples."

"And yet you will need them. I'd suggest you follow their direction if you want to stay safe."

Her jaw dropped. "Um, listen, you might be a

goddess, but I'm human. As in not involved in your"—she waved a hand—"religious stuff and all. I'd really rather not be dragged into something."

"As if you have a choice." Hekate's laughter tinkled. "Time for you to return to your time and place, but know you can rest easy for I've sent you my two very best. They will take good care of you."

Before Adeline could say boo, she blinked and there she was still standing on the sidewalk with Ambrose.

"You met Hekate," he stated in the face of her dazed expression.

"That or I had a very vivid hallucination." Could it be the tofu? She'd managed a bite before the interruption.

His lips twitched. "It is a bit strange the first time. But I assure you, of the many gods out there, Hekate is one of the good ones."

"As if you'd say anything else," she drawled.

"Do you believe me now?"

"I guess." Even Adeline couldn't deny something had just happened. "But what I don't understand is why I'd need protection. And from a goddess, no less." Two goddesses, supposedly. Why would Mother Earth be interested in her?

He shrugged. "Alas, Hekate didn't say. But given the events we've seen thus far, I'd say it won't be long before we discern our purpose."

"What events? A single wererat isn't a big deal."

"And the guy in the restaurant?"

"Having a mental crisis."

"If you say so."

They'd reached her stoop, and she paused. "I guess you'll be heading back for Orion."

"And insult him? No thanks. I am, however, hoping you'll invite me in."

The request had her staring at him. For one, she still didn't know him well—and what she did know about him being an agent turned out to be a lie. Two, he'd take up a lot of space in her tiny place, and if she found him titillating out in the open, how intense would it be then? Three, it had been a while since she'd been alone with a guy, especially one that had her tingling.

A woman her age knew better than to invite a stranger into her place.

But a lonely woman didn't have many opportunities and had learned to trust her gut. A gut that didn't sense any danger from him.

"Would you like to come in?"

"Yes, thank you." At least he had excellent manners. Here was to hoping he didn't turn out to be a serial killer.

She let him into the apartment to find her cats still guarding the bathroom door. It drew Ambrose's attention.

"Are they always that interested in your washroom?"

"No. But they're cats, so who knows what goes through their furry minds?" Ambrose paced to the cats, who ignored him. The three then stared inside her small bathroom, which she'd at least cleaned the day before. Hopefully she hadn't left any underwear on the floor.

"Can I get you a coffee?" she asked, suddenly nervous now that he was in her place.

"Yes, please."

As she busied herself, he moved from the bathroom doorway and took a spot on one of her two kitchen chairs that went with the small bistro table. She didn't remember the last time she'd had a guest sitting at it.

"How long have you lived here?" he asked.

"A few years. I got evicted from my last place after the first attempted home invasion."

"It's an old building," he remarked.

"It is, which means it has its quirks." She glanced to her staring cats. "Like plumbing that sometimes releases bugs." She held in a shudder. The coffee finished percolating, and she carried over a cup, along with a carton of almond milk and a bowl of sugar.

"Thanks."

"You're welcome." Stuck in an uncomfortable loop of politeness. How should she break it? She took a sip before saying, "Should you be checking on Orion?"

"He's fine."

"How can you know that?" she queried with a frown.

He tapped his temple. "Hekate would let me know if he required my aid."

"Oh." Then because she found herself curious. "How does one become a helper for a god?"

"Some do it via worship, others inherit it from a family member. In our case, we chose to not steal from a witch who was a disciple of Hekate."

"You're thieves?" She couldn't help the lilted question.

"Not anymore and, at the time, we did it out of desperation. We were orphaned and starving. The goddess took pity on us and offered us a more honest way of living."

"So you enjoy being her lackeys?" Such a strange conversation to be having.

"It has its perks. Always fed. Clothed. Housed. Plus, we get to travel."

"What does your wife think?" Yeah, that wasn't exactly subtle, and she was okay with it, given Adeline never wanted to be the other woman.

"Not married," he offered with a smile. "Never found the right person, but I keep hoping." Said while staring at her.

She ducked her head and eyed her coffee. "I'm single too."

"Surprising."

The reply had her snorting. "Not really. Guess I should warn you I'm kind of bad luck. People tend to die around me."

"Unless you're killing them, not sure how that's your fault."

"Except I worry it is somehow because of me." She

shrugged as she admitted something she'd long kept tight to her chest. "I mean some of the ways I've lost friends have been something out of a movie. The kind people call unrealistic."

"Accidents happen."

"But they seem to be really common around me. Anyhow, thought I should mention it. I could be hazardous to your health."

"I would have said my heart," he murmured, startling her.

"You have a heart condition?"

Laughter burst from him. "No, I meant more the fact that it races when you're around."

"It does?" She gaped at him in surprise.

"I'm sorry. I'm being much too forward."

"No, it's okay. It's just I'm not usually the type to inspire passion or..." She waved a hand. "Let's just say, I'm not the kind of woman who makes men go crazy."

"Then they are blind. You are extremely sexy, smart, and fun to be around."

Her cheeks heated as she answered with, "How can you say that when we've barely spoken?"

"We're speaking right now."

Indeed, they were, and already she'd enjoyed herself more than she had on pretty much any first date. "Are scions allowed to date?"

"Yes, as well as marry and have children."

"What about your job for the goddess?"

"The goddess wants only what's best for us. If we

were to fall in love, she'd adjust her expectation of us in regard to our duty."

"Must be nice to actually talk to your boss."

"Oh, is yours often absent?"

"More like never even met in person. I was hired over the phone and told my duties. Only other folks I've met are the elven night crew."

"How long have you been employed there?"

"Almost two decades now."

"And you've never met the owner?" Incredulity laced his reply.

"I know, weird, right? Which is why when you showed up, I assumed you were investigating my boss, but then you told me you weren't actually CA, that you're here for me, which still makes no sense. I'm nothing special—"

She never finished speaking because suddenly he was in front of her, his lips pressing against hers with a whispered, "You are indeed very special."

And so was he. She tingled head to toe at the embrace, and as the kiss deepened, she parted her lips for his tongue.

Before she knew it, he'd drawn her from the chair into his arms, his body solid and warm against hers, his lips firm and, at the same time, sensually coaxing. Her breath shortened, and every inch of her tingled. When his hands slid from her back to her waist then cupped her butt, she was ready to drag him to her couch.

Only someone pounded at the door.

Ambrose released her reluctantly, and she fought to regain some measure of composure. It would have helped if her knees didn't want to buckle.

What a kiss.

"It's Orion," he announced grimly. His long stride took exactly two steps to reach the door and fling it open.

A disheveled Orion stood there, not wearing the clothes she'd last seen him in. At least, she didn't remember the bright pink tank top or tight gray shorts.

"What happened?" Ambrose asked.

Orion glanced past him to Adeline and shook his head, whispering something.

Ambrose tossed her a quick glance. "Give us a second."

They exited the apartment, and she was left to mull over what just happened.

He kissed me!

Surprise-kissed. Which she had to admit she loved. Most guys these days asked permission, which kind of took the fun out of it. But Ambrose, he acted with passion, and wow... She wondered how far things would have gone if they'd not been interrupted.

Rowr.

A glance at her cats showed their hackles rising.

"What is it? Did the icky bug crawl out of the drain?" She headed over to see, even as she'd rather not know what multi-legged monstrosity had her felines agitated.

The cats arched their backs and hissed, unusual even for them. They usually only acted that way when—

Adeline abruptly whirled and darted for her purse with the taser. As her hands gripped it, she heard a wet plopping sound.

And a much deeper growl.

She turned to face the bathroom more slowly, jaw-dropping at the sight of Smudge and Fudge, only they were about a zillion times bigger than usual.

But they weren't why she froze in shock.

That would be the octopus-like creature that gripped the edge of the doorway and heaved itself into view!

CHAPTER 9

An agitated Orion paced the sidewalk in his ill-fitting clothes, snagged on his way over. He'd seen a guy about to enter a boxing gym and tore his fitness bag out of his hands. He'd changed in an alley before making his way to Adeline's place.

Ambrose joined him, huffing, "What happened?"

"The military. That's what fucking happened," Orion grumbled, clenching his fists. "I detained the guy accosting Adeline, and was about to march him up the street to the truck to ask some questions, when they came busting in."

"Hold on. Did you say the military?" Ambrose blinked in surprise.

"Or some kind of similar type group. They wore black fatigues, helmets with blacked-out visors, and came armed to the teeth. They screamed at everyone to hit the floor. Seeing as how I wasn't about to get caught in a sweep, I shifted and bolted through the kitchen and out the back door. However, I did stick around long enough to see them shoving the guy into a van and questioning the people inside before swinging an amulet in their faces."

"Why would the military be making arrests?" Ambrose asked, rubbing his chin.

"I don't know. Given they sent some of their guys looking for me, I didn't stick around to find out."

"It's got to be related to the reason why Hekate wants us here," Ambrose mused aloud. "Did you get a good sniff of the guy accosting Adeline? Sense anything off?"

"Do you mean was he dead like the wererat?" Orion shrugged. "No clue if he was missing his soul, but there was something off about him."

"Off how?"

"The way his eyes didn't fully focus, and he kept saying 'I need it back. I feel so empty.'"

"Adeline claims she's never seen him before."

"Did—"

A loud yowl drew their attention.

"Fuck!" Orion didn't stop to think, he reacted, leaping from the sidewalk into the stairwell before slamming into the apartment. He abruptly froze in place, mostly because he tried to grasp what he saw.

Tentacles, as it turned out. Many tentacles, wrapped around the oversized cats, and Adeline! For the second time in less than an hour, he shifted, bursting out of his clothes and throwing himself, teeth first, to clamp onto the nearest appendage.

It had a rubbery, slimy texture to it, and when he bit down hard, he severed flesh. It didn't have much effect, other than the stump spewed a nasty-smelling ichor. It also didn't stop other tentacles from reaching for him. Did this thing not feel pain?

It hit him in that moment that, despite the impossibility, he beheld a kraken. Completely unheard of but it explained the gaping maw. It couldn't breathe without water, and yet it remained determined to attack.

Adeline yelled, "Taser. Floor." A directive not aimed at Orion the hound, but Ambrose, who bent down and snagged it. However, his friend hesitated to use the weapon, and Orion immediately grasped why. If he zapped the kraken, he'd also be zapping Adeline since it had her in its grip.

Orion uttered a snarl and dove at the arm wrapped around her lower half, gnawing through the rubbery flesh. The odor and taste reminded him why he didn't care for sushi.

"Zap it," screamed Adeline. "It's crushing my kitties!"

"Get her loose. I'll help the cats," Ambrose hollered. He pulled a small knife from his pocket that extended into a foot-long dagger when he shook it, the faint pink glow of magic fading immediately. As Ambrose slashed at the arms holding the cats, Orion tore into the tentacle trying to drag Adeline to the wide-open mouth of the beast.

Not today, sushi. Despite the bad taste in his mouth,

Orion chomped the rubbery tentacle, crunching partway through before another appendage slapped him off. He scrabbled onto his four paws and headed back for Adeline, only Ambrose got there first and freed her with a slash of his dagger.

Adeline stumbled free and yelled, "Kill it!"

Ambrose extended the taser but frowned when it didn't go off, leading Adeline to grab it from his hand and fire it.

The kraken uttered a keening sound and shivered. Its whole body jiggled and wobbled before exploding into chunks. Pieces of gore and flesh slapped them in the face.

"Ew. Gross. Darn it." Adeline wiped her gory face with her equally dirty shirt.

Orion yipped while mentally saying, *"Did it come alone?"*

Ambrose stuck his head in the bathroom. "No sign of any other critters. Looks like it squeezed through the tub drain."

"Explains why Smudge and Fudge were watching so intently," Adeline's wooden response to the claim as shock set in.

Despite the grossness, Orion sniffed the remains. They smelled off. Slightly rancid. Or should he say, dead?

"What am I going to do?" Adeline wailed as she surveilled the destruction. "My landlord is going to freak."

The landlord wouldn't be the only one. The neighbors would likely cause a stink, too, because Orion doubted the ruckus went unnoticed.

In the midst of the chaos, the cats shrank back down to kitty-size and began to lick themselves clean. No way would Orion be tonguing his fur.

The monster's shredded remains were gag-worthy, and the mess epic in size, but neither was the reason why Ambrose stated, "We have to get out of here."

His advice came about because of the blinking device buried in the flesh.

A tracking device. Someone had sent that kraken to find her.

CHAPTER 10

"Excuse me?" Adeline exclaimed in response to Ambrose's declaration they should leave.

"We have to go. Like, now," he insisted.

Adeline shook her head. "I can't leave. I have to clean this icky mess up before it permanently ruins my things."

"We don't have time. This was no accident." Ambrose pointed to a blinking light embedded in the bulkier part of the carcass.

"What is that?" she asked dumbly.

"Tracking device, which means we're going to have company. Soon, I'd wager."

"I don't understand. Why would a sewer monster have a tracking device?" And how the heck had it squeezed up through her pipes?

"We don't have the luxury of time to figure it out." Ambrose held out his hand. "We really have to go."

On the one hand, Adeline understood his urgency.

On the other, she didn't want to leave her apartment. This was her home. Her safety. Or at least it used to be.

Meow. A furry head nudged her hand, and she looked down to see Smudge peering at her.

Fudge rubbed against her from behind. Her cats were encouraging her to follow Ambrose, who stood at the door, a handsome capable man who'd rushed to her rescue.

And then there was Orion… the dog. He'd also dove in to protect her.

As did her cats.

Cats that could grow to the size of ponies.

As her world toppled, a faint feeling flooded all her muscles, along with nausea. Her knees buckled, and she hit the floor.

"We don't have time for you to be having an episode," Orion grumbled, scooping her in his arms. Naked arms that tucked her to a naked chest.

It snapped her out of some of her stupor. "Why are you not wearing clothes?"

"Because I lost them in the shift."

Made sense. And didn't. In her world, men didn't turn into dogs. Then again, monsters also didn't come slithering out of her tub.

Orion carried her out while Ambrose led the way, her cats slinking alongside. He extended his key fob, and the lights on the SUV blinked. "Get in the back with Adeline. I'll drive."

Ambrose flung open the rear passenger door, but

before Orion could toss Adeline in, Fudge and Smudge leapt onto the leather seats.

Adeline slid in after them, and then Orion squished against her, all naked six-feet-plus of him. It was hard to look away, but she did, cheeks hot, which she liked better than the bone-chilling cold of before.

What had just happened? Why would an octopus with a tracking device come after her? It made no sense.

The vehicle lurched into motion and turned down a street almost right away. "Where are we going?"

"We're renting a house nearby." Ambrose glanced at her via the rearview mirror. "It's halfway between your work and home to provide an easy base of operation for our mission."

"A mission to guard me," she repeated dully. "Guess you succeeded. The octopus is dead."

"That was a kraken, which are a tad smarter than an octopus. More dangerous, too. I've never heard of one leaving the water before," Ambrose explained, but Adeline didn't care. Octopus, kraken. Neither should have been in her apartment.

"Think it was following orders?" Orion asked.

The inanity had Adeline snorting. "Pretty sure a kraken isn't taking instructions from anyone. Most likely it was in a zoo or privately owned and escaped, hence the tracker. And now that you've saved me, I guess your goddess will have you moving on."

At her statement, Ambrose shook his head. "I doubt this is the last of the danger."

"Danger to me? Like, why? I'm a nobody." She rubbed her forehead. A nudge to her arm showed Smudge wanting some pets. The strokes over the fur did much to soothe until she remembered mega-Smudge and mega-Fudge. Had some survival instinct kicked in to make them huge? Did she care? Not really, since Smudge crept into her lap.

Nice kitty. And it only took a near-death seafood experience.

"We're here," Ambrose announced. "Hold on while I get us inside where we can't be seen."

The townhouse-style home had an automatic garage door that lifted to give entry and then closed behind them.

It took Orion opening the door of the SUV for her to realize that while she'd been petting the cat with one hand, her other gripped his bare thigh.

"Sorry." She turned her head, blushing, especially once she realized how close she was to his groin.

"You can grab me anytime," Orion promised. He turned around and held out a hand to help her out, unbothered by his nudity—and with good reason. *Oh my.* She averted her gaze but not before she saw his penis twitch and grow.

Even bigger. *Oh my.*

Fudge and Smudge leapt to the ground with no problem and waited for someone to give them access to the house. The interior garage door led to a small vestibule for the main entrance, with a closet and a sign on a closed door marked utility room. They headed for the stairs going up.

Ambrose led the way, a good thing because she might have been distracted if she'd had to stare at Orion's naked ass. Might have even drooled a bit. The man had a very fine physique. It now made her wish she'd flirted more. Wait, was she allowed to think that after kissing his partner?

Upon entering the main level of the house, which gleamed white—kitchen cabinets, countertops, white tile floor, and in the living room area, white leather couches and carpet—Adeline froze. "I'm too filthy to be in here. I'll stain something for sure."

"Don't worry about it. If we lose the cleaning deposit, so be it. We all need a scrub. There's only two showers. Since you and Orion are dirtiest, you go first. Orion, you take the hall bath. Adeline, you can have the master."

"I can't walk on the carpet." Her feet were covered in kraken slime.

"I've got you." Ambrose ditched his mucky shoes for his clean socks and held out his arms. Look at her being a princess carried twice in one day. She might have enjoyed it more if not so traumatized.

He lugged her up the stairs right into a large bedchamber with a huge bed. So that was what king-sized must mean. Did he and Orion share it? She didn't get the impression they were lovers, not with the way they'd both flirted with her.

The bathroom, like the kitchen, gleamed white and

clean, the tiles shiny and new-looking. Ambrose started the shower with one hand, still holding her against him.

She leaned her head on his shoulder and sighed. "What an evening."

"It has been somewhat interesting," he agreed. "Glad we got to kiss before it went to hell."

That lifted her head. "Really?"

He smiled down at her. "Yes, really. I am hoping we can continue it once you've recovered from the ordeal."

Would it sound crazy if she claimed she was ready now? A kiss might make her forget the horror of her apartment. She settled for, "I'd like that."

"If I set you on your feet, can you stand long enough to undress and shower, or do you need my help?"

How tempting to have him strip her. Touch her.

She tingled with desire but, at the same time, shuddered. Covered in kraken guts wasn't the time for passionate thoughts or acts.

"I think I can manage."

"Holler if you need me." He left her in the bathroom with the steaming shower, and for a second, she almost called him back. All of a sudden, her arms felt heavy, her fingers leaden.

Shock set in, and it took her a few fumbling seconds to get off her shirt then her pants and undergarments. The entire time she trembled.

I could have died.

Sure, she'd been attacked before but never had she actually thought she'd be killed. She'd always easily come ahead. If it hadn't been for Ambrose and Orion...

Before she could collapse under the weight of her own thoughts, she stood under the hot spray. The pounding warmth eased the chill nestled in her bones, and as she relaxed, she sighed.

I'm alive.

Her apartment might be a write-off, and she'd probably end up evicted, but she'd emerged from that scary moment unscathed. It did, however, leave her with lots of questions, and she knew who might have the answers.

The fluffy towel proved large enough it could almost wrap around her twice. A smaller one provided a turban for her hair. A glance at her clothes had her wrinkling her nose. She couldn't put those back on. Maybe she could borrow something from the guys.

She emerged from the bathroom to find Ambrose changed into a clean outfit and lounging on the bed. An equally relaxed Orion, wearing only track pants, sprawled beside him, his hair still damp.

She paused because they provided quite the visual tableaux. A more sexually confident woman might have dropped the towel and seen what happened, but Adeline wrapped her arms around herself and muttered, "I don't have anything to wear."

"If you ask me, you're wearing too much." Orion winked.

Ambrose cuffed Orion. "Now is not the time. She's been through an ordeal."

"It's okay." She offered a wan smile.

"You look like you're feeling better," Orion stated.

"I wouldn't say better so much as not gross." She grimaced. "That was very unpleasant. I've never been attacked by something like that before. And never had to deal with such a mess. Usually, I zap with a taser, maybe give it a whack for good measure, and it's over."

"Not many people have faced a beast like that and lived to tell the tale. Luckily it was a young kraken, or we'd have been really screwed. Mature adults have been known to take down ships." Ambrose, the walking encyclopedia for monsters.

"I can't believe it managed to squeeze itself up through that tub drain."

"Not so farfetched if you've ever watched an octopus video. They can squeeze through the tiniest of gaps." Orion's turn to share bits of knowledge.

"I think it might be time to think of getting an apartment that's not on the ground level," her reply. Screw the cheap rent. Past time she took better steps to protect herself.

"Speaking of apartment..." Ambrose paused.

"What of it?"

Orion rolled from the bed and held out a phone. "It's not being mentioned on the news, but I managed to save a video posted on social media before it got scrubbed."

She grabbed his device and stared at the shaky

video, taken from a few floors above her place. A trio of black vans came screeching to a halt in front of her building and men in combat gear emerged with guns out. They rushed down the stoop, and while she couldn't see what happened next, they must have entered her place given how many disappeared. They emerged not long after, one with a baggie holding the flashing device. Others had armfuls of her things.

Her mouth rounded. "Why are they taking my stuff?"

"To find out who you are," Ambrose's grim reply.

"But I did nothing wrong. I acted in self-defense."

"This isn't about the kraken. Or the wererat. This is about something bigger."

"No." She shook her head and handed back the phone. "They must have the wrong person."

"Or maybe there's something about you that's special, but hidden," Ambrose suggested.

"I'm almost forty. Don't you think I'd have noticed by now?"

Before the men could reply, Smudge sauntered in, tail high, looking cocky.

Adeline pointed. "Is it me, or did my cats get mega-sized back at the apartment?"

Ambrose and Orion glanced at each other before the latter said, "Your cats have been god-blessed. I'm thinking by Gaia most likely."

"Wait, so they're not cats?" She struggled to understand.

"They are, but they've been enhanced to provide you with protection."

She stared at him then Smudge. "That can't be right. I've had them for years, and they've never done that before."

"Because you usually handled threats on your own. Most likely they were instructed to be discreet."

Her lips pursed. "You know, the more I spend time with you guys, the more my life is unravelling. Next thing you know, you'll tell me my job isn't real and a god gave it to me so I could pay rent."

"It's a possibility, given the protections around your sandwich shop." Ambrose offered the possibility with a shrug.

"Don't you think if that hex were for me it'd also be around my apartment?" Ha, she had him there.

"They can't spell your building because its very structure nullifies magic," Ambrose countered.

"How would you know that?"

"Because I tried to install a hex of watchfulness the first day we arrived, and it was gone within the hour." Ambrose shrugged. "It's not entirely uncommon. Many humans aren't comfortable with magic, and so they built edifices to block it."

"Well, that explains a few things," she muttered. Such as why the few magical trinkets she brought home always stopped working. She glanced at Smudge. "How come it didn't affect my cats?"

"Blessings aren't magic. They are genetic changes to a body."

She sighed. "This is exhausting."

Ambrose patted the bed. "Then come lie down."

She stared at him. "With you?"

"Given what's happened, it would be best if you weren't left alone."

"How would anything find me here?"

"How did the kraken and rat find you at home?"

Good point. She glanced at Orion, wondering what he'd think of her sleeping with Ambrose.

He winked. "Don't worry about me, sweetheart. I lost rock, paper, scissors and got stuck with first watch. But fear not, I'll be by for a snuggle later."

Her mouth went dry, and then she wrung her hands. Ambrose had kissed her. She really should set him straight, only Orion left before she could say anything.

"What's wrong? You look sick."

She glanced at him. "I shouldn't be sharing a bed with Orion, given you and I kissed. It wouldn't be right."

"Would it help if I said he was my best friend?"

"Meaning what? Do you usually share w-w-women?" she stuttered, mostly because she didn't know what to say. Blame her frazzled nerves.

"No, we've never shared sexual partners, but then again, we've both never been interested in the same woman before."

"You're both interested in me?" she squeaked. Yes, they'd flirted, but they were guys. Guys did that, and it didn't always mean anything.

"Very much so, and while at first I was a tad hesitant, I can't think of anything more right than sharing someone very special with my best friend."

"I don't know if I'm into that kind of thing." Her honest reply, which came with hot cheeks.

"We don't have to indulge in a three-way if you're not comfortable, but what if we took turns pleasing you?" he murmured.

She wanted to huff she wasn't a whore, but at the same time, his suggestion had her tingling, her pulse racing. The thought of having these two virile men as her lovers... That kind of thing happened to other people, not middle-aged Adeline who worked at a nowhere job and whose idea of a fun Friday was *Star Trek* reruns.

"Come to bed." He patted the mattress once more, and this time she padded slowly to him, only to realize she still wore only a towel. "I need something to wear."

"Here." He sat up and stripped off his shirt, revealing a muscled torso that had her suddenly weak in the knees.

In a flash, he stood by her, steadying her. "Easy there. You've had a rough night. Let me help you."

She could only stand dumbly as his deft fingers stripped the towel from her body and then encased her in his shirt, still warm from his body. He then carried her to bed and tucked her under the covers. All that and not a single attempt to grope.

Not knowing what to expect, she held still as he

climbed into bed with her. Would he stay on his side? Ask permission to cuddle? Or...

He slid close, laid an arm over her, and nuzzled her hair, whispering, "Go to sleep. You're safe."

More than that, she felt cared for, a strange and welcome sensation. At the same time, now that the shock had worn off, she couldn't help but think of his kiss. A kiss that had made her feel so alive.

And she wanted that really badly right now. A reminder that she wasn't being digested in a kraken's belly.

She wiggled her bottom to get close to him. His arm tightened to tuck her against his body. His erection pressed against her backside.

The arm draped over her shifted, and his hand went from palming her belly to sliding upward. He cupped her breast, squeezing it, and he shifted her hair aside to kiss her nape.

She sighed and shivered as pleasurable tingles spread through her body.

Was she being wanton? Yes. Did she care? No. She'd never been the type to be casual or take risks. But if anyone deserved it today, it was her. So when he tugged up his shirt and his hand began teasing her mound, she rolled to her back to give him access.

He slid a finger between her parted thighs, stroking her, drawing little gasps. She could feel her own juices slicking his digit as he rubbed it over her clit. He stopped for a moment to tug the shirt higher, baring her breasts. Regular breasts, not too small or big, the nipples already erect. He sucked on the tip of one while his finger stroked her.

She mewled, her hips rolling, excitement making her needy.

When he repositioned himself between her legs, she was ready for him to take her, only he slid down low and dipped his head.

Wait, what? Men rarely went down on her, even though she enjoyed it. Most were interested in getting off as quick as they could.

Not Ambrose.

At his first lick, she arched. By the second and third, she was grabbing the sheets and writhing. He inserted a finger then two as he lapped at her clit, teasing her.

Building her pleasure.

Tightening her body.

She came silently, mouth open wide, but nothing came out as an orgasm rolled through her, intense enough to leave her trembling.

She expected him to take his turn as she came down from her high, but he ended up behind her again, snuggling her close and whispering, "Sweet dreams, sweetheart."

To her surprise, she slept soundly and woke to a different man in bed.

CHAPTER 11

ORION HATED TAKING FIRST WATCH AND MISSING OUT ON some alone time with Adeline, but at the same time, it was probably for the best given Ambrose had been leery about his suggestion when it came to sharing. Not something they'd ever done before but Orion had a feeling about Adeline. A feeling she was that special person they'd both been waiting for. Could he convince Ambrose and her of it, though? It helped that he knew Ambrose found himself attracted to her. There'd been no hiding the proof.

Upon arriving at their rental, Orion had showered quickly before seeking out Ambrose to say, "You kissed her."

His friend had looked chagrinned as he admitted, "I did."

"You knew I was interested in her," Orion stated, not with any anger, more just a reminder.

"I know, and yet I find myself also attracted." A quiet admission.

"I wish I could tell you good luck and stand by; however, I'm pretty sure she's the one." Not a thing Orion expected to ever say.

Ambrose sighed. "I've got the same feeling as you. I don't think I can walk away."

"Why should either of us give up? With all we've been through, could you think of anything better than us both sharing the love of the same woman?"

This led to Ambrose making a face. "I've told you before I'm not interested in your dick."

Orion chuckled. "No offense, but neither am I. What I'm talking about isn't an orgy but rather an understanding that we can both care for and be with her. No jealousy. No games. Just two best friends taking turns with the one woman in the world that is perfect for us." Orion had never been more certain of that fact. And he should know.

He'd been with hundreds of women. Never had one enthralled him like Adeline. He couldn't even pinpoint what it was exactly. The excellent sandwich helped. As did her looks. But seeing her bravely ready to confront that wererat and then, with the kraken, boldly using her taser instead of running and screaming... He'd wanted nothing more in that moment than to drag her into his arms and kiss her. And protect her. And hug her. If he didn't think she'd kick him in the balls, he'd have joined her in that shower. He didn't know how Ambrose managed to leave that room knowing she was in there naked.

At his words, Ambrose had dipped his head for a moment before saying, "In the past, I've worried that one day a relationship might tear us apart or change our dynamic."

"Same." Ambrose was more than a friend. Orion would have given his life to save Ambrose, and he knew his partner would do the same.

"I don't know if Adeline will go for it, though," Ambrose murmured, glancing at the master bedroom door. "Threesomes are still considered somewhat taboo."

"I think it will depend on how we present it. We let her know it's not about having an orgy but about two men caring for her. The orgy can come later," Orion added with a wink.

"We'll see about that," Ambrose's dry reply.

"It might never happen. To start, if she's willing, I'm thinking we handle it like those dudes on TV shows with a ton of wives. They have scheduled nights with each woman."

"A schedule? Doesn't sound romantic." Ambrose grimaced.

Orion laughed. "I'm not saying we need to get that extreme, but we take turns. Like tonight, for example. One of us should stand watch while the other gets some sleep with her. Maybe get the ball rolling... if you know what I mean."

Ambrose blushed. "She's gone through a trauma,

and she barely knows me. I hardly think she'll be in the mood."

"She kissed you."

"Actually, I kissed her."

"But she liked it. So, do it again. I'm not saying have wild sex, but cuddling and a little petting... Put her at ease."

"You do realize if I do that first, she might not let you touch her after. She seems to be the type to be loyal."

"Which is why you'll need to pave the way, explain how we both feel, see how she responds."

"And if she says no?"

Orion grinned. "You really think she'll be able to resist us both?"

After that discussion, Ambrose took alone time with Adeline first and Orion kept watch, his keen hearing not missing her sounds of pleasure. Some might have been jealous. He got hard. In his heart, he knew this was the way. The way to remain partnered with Ambrose. The way to a future where love was possible. Maybe even kids someday.

First, though, they had to figure out the mystery around Adeline.

As he paced between the front window of the place and the back, watching for movement or anything suspicious, he placed a call to a friend at the Ottawa CA, routing his cellular data through an app to hide his location. Could never be too cautious.

Bertha answered with a cheery, "If it isn't my favorite himbo."

"A himbo who failed to seduce you," he teased.

"Not my fault you won't trade that dick in for a sweet pussy."

"Alas, I am quite attached to it."

His reply had Bertha laughing. "What's up? What are you meddling in now?" They'd been acquainted for years and she knew who he worked for. He'd once helped her out of a bind with an ex-lover, a witch who'd been setting curses after they broke up and needed a stern reminder that Hekate didn't approve of her magic being used in such a fashion.

"What makes you think I'm not just calling to chat with my favorite CA agent?" he teased.

"Because when you want to chat, you show up at my office and drag me to the nearest bar to do shots."

True. "Will have to do that next time I'm in town. But you're right. I did call with an ulterior motive. I witnessed something strange today and wondered if you'd heard about it."

"You'll have to be more explicit."

"Bunch of unmarked black vans with military-dressed dudes converged on a restaurant and arrested a guy."

"And? Sounds like a human operation."

"Those same vans and people also confiscated a wererat taken into CA custody in the Montreal office and then wiped all mention of it."

He heard a chair squeak, and Bertha's voice

lowered as she replied, "What the hell did you get involved in?"

"I don't know."

"Is this a goddess mission?"

"Yes, but it came with no information. Do you know anything?"

He could barely hear her whispered, "Those vans and the people in them in combat gear have been spotted all around Montreal, but no one seems to know who they work for. While I didn't know about the restaurant incident, I did hear about the rat. A girl I used to hook up with gave me a shout as they were invading the office. She hung up, and when I called her later, she didn't remember a thing."

"You say they've been all over the city?"

"Yeah. People have been recording and posting them on social media with all kinds of conspiracy theories. Those videos have been coming down as fast as they go up, meaning someone with deep pockets is trying to keep it quiet."

"Government?" he queried.

"Very possible. Most likely one of their secret divisions."

"Since when are they allowed to meddle in cryptid affairs?"

"They're not," Bertha's flat reply. "But given they had the authority to go in and take the wererat, seems to me they've got some kind of agreement in place."

"Any idea what they're looking for?" He didn't

mention what he knew of the wererat's less-than-alive status.

"Nope. And I didn't poke, seeing as they're messing with people's memories."

On a whim, he asked, "Can you find out information on a sandwich shop owner for me?"

"Going to file a complaint because they didn't give you enough meat?"

He snickered. "I've got all the extra meat I need. More seriously, there's something off about the owner of this place. I think they're probably cryptid but very secretive. Maybe using the shop as a front for something."

"What's the name?"

He gave her the information but before hanging up said, "I don't have to tell you to keep this quiet."

"Of course I'll be quiet. Anything to stay off the 'to be mind-wiped' list. Dude, if some weird shit is going down that involves cryptids, then I should know about it." Bertha being in charge of human and cryptid relations for Canada.

"Be careful."

"Now that's no fun," drawled Bertha.

Orion hung up and pondered the mysterious folks in combat gear. They'd been allowed to walk into a CA office without issue, meaning they must be working with or had higher authority. Were they cryptid? He'd not been able to tell given the armor they wore.

As he paced from front window to back, he noticed one of Adeline's cats watching him. "I'm thinking we're probably safe here for a few hours. If I pop out, can you keep watch and wake them if something comes?"

The cat's eyes glowed green for a second, and it nodded.

Fair enough. While it might not be the best idea to leave, he found himself too curious to sit still. He exited the house and flipped to his canine self in the deepest shadow he could find before trotting off.

The rental truly did sit midway between Adeline's apartment and work. He headed for her place first, curious if the soldiers remained on site. He arrived to find the block quiet. Eerily so. He remained across the street observing, not sure what raised his hackles. It took several minutes before he noticed motion in the window of her place. A pair of night vision goggles peeked out.

Where there was one, there would be—

Zap.

The magical spell struck, and had he been an ordinary shifter or dog, he would have fallen, but Hekate had blessed Orion, and so he absorbed the magic and whirled to see two helmeted guys readying to throw another spell bomb.

He lunged, taking the first down as his buddy splatted Orion with another hex. He crunched the helmet of the guy he'd toppled, which wouldn't kill but did result in some screaming. He'd scream, too, if a tin can got crushed around his head.

When he heard a gun leave its holster, he spun

with a growl and advanced on the fellow who took aim. He dodged as the guy fired, fast enough to get away with only a furrow along his flank before he barreled into the marksman.

They hit the ground hard, the helmet bouncing off the ground, leaving the guy limp. Orion grabbed the visor with his teeth and tore it off, revealing a human face and an unmistakable human scent. A fucking human? What were they doing fucking with cryptids?

The first guy began to shout, "B team needs backup," indicating more troops in the area. Time to leave, but before Orion ran off, he snagged the guy's utility belt and tugged hard enough the buckle snapped. It jiggled and bounced as he raced, the shouts behind him fading as he put distance between them. Being a smart hound, he didn't run in the direction of the rental but away from it, ensuring he lost his pursuers before he took a roundabout route that passed the sandwich shop.

A glance in showed elves at work, a good number of them. Expensive for a store that didn't generate much revenue. Also odd that they could enter, given the cryptid-repelling spell. Perhaps they had a hex to counter or a secret entrance.

He made it back to the house and shifted, striding in naked with his prize to find Ambrose standing there with an arched brow.

"And where were you?" his friend asked.

"Checking on Adeline's place. Those men in black were still watching it. Two of them jumped me."

"Did you kill them?" Ambrose queried, trying to find out if they'd have to do some damage control.

"They were alive when I left. I got this." Orion held up the belt.

"Let's see what we've got." Ambrose snatched it and headed for the kitchen counter while Orion threw on his pants. He less than casually asked, "How did it go?"

Ambrose got a tight secretive smile. "Fine."

"Sounded like more than fine," he grumbled.

"Oh, that. She needed some stress relief."

"And?"

"I broached the idea of her dating both of us. She seemed receptive."

"Really?" Relief flooded him.

"Yes, but take it slow. It's one thing to talk about it, another to actually do it."

"I'm aware. I'll be patient." He couldn't help grinning.

Ambrose bent over the tool belt and examined it. "Military issue." He pointed to the manufacturing label inside it. "All of it is." He pointed to the various pouches.

Orion neared and gave it a sniff. "I smell magic."

Opening the pockets revealed more of the sleep bombs, plus some he didn't recognize, but his partner did. "Flashbang hexes."

"What's this?" Orion pulled out a remote control with only a few buttons. A red one, yellow, and blue.

"No idea, but don't push any. Hand it over."

Ambrose flipped it over and slid off the back to remove the batteries. "Just in case."

"Fuck, you think they could track it?" Orion could have slapped himself.

Ambrose shook his head. "It's not emitting a signal, so it should be fine." The rest of the pockets didn't reveal much. A knife, zip ties, a pack of gum, and a crumpled receipt.

"It's for a corner store," Orion remarked. "Guy bought gum, a coffee, and smokes."

"What's the address?" Ambrose punched it into his phone and then zoomed in. "It's by an industrial area."

"Could that be where they're hiding out when they're not taking wererats and random weird dudes into custody?"

"Maybe. I'll see if I can pull up any aerial footage," Ambrose stated as Orion yawned.

His friend glanced at him. "Go get some sleep."

"Okay, I'll be in the spare room if you need me."

"Sleep in the master."

"You think she'd be okay with that?" Orion hesitated, a strange thing for him. However, he couldn't get this thing with Adeline wrong.

"Guess we'll find out."

Hence why he slid into a bed with a warm and snuggly body. Not that he mauled her. Orion lay beside Adeline watching her sleep. Hoping she wouldn't push him away.

Dreaming of what could be...

CHAPTER 12

Adeline woke to find Orion asleep beside her, his face vulnerable in repose. Handsome too. Looking at him made her think of what Ambrose had said, about taking them both as lovers.

Much too soon to contemplate. She'd only barely met them.

Yet she'd let Ambrose pleasure her to climax. What if Orion wanted to do the same?

Such a slutty thing to contemplate.

Also very titillating.

At the same time, how could she even dare to think she could satisfy not one but two incredible hunks?

It would be exciting to try.

If it was real. What if she dreamed?

Orion opened his eyes. "Good morning, sweetheart."

"Hey," her soft reply.

"Did you sleep okay?"

She nodded and wondered if he knew what she and Ambrose had done. She bit her lower lip.

"Don't you go being all shy on me. I know you and Ambrose fooled around, and I'm cool with it. He says he talked to you a bit about the fact we're both interested in you."

"Yeah, but I'm not sure how to feel about it." Embarrassed, for one. She never actually thought people had discussions about that kind of thing. Heck, she never thought anyone would propose it to her.

"Do you like us?"

"Yes, but I also barely know you."

"Which is why dating exists."

"Date both of you?"

"Don't think of us as two separate people. Me and Ambrose, we're a team. We've shared everything since a young age."

"Even women?" she had to ask.

"Nope. You'd be the first and only because you're special."

Her nose scrunched. "Not really."

"You are to us. And we'd really like to show you how much if you'll let us."

"By having a threesome," she stated, the words blurting out from her lips.

"By doing whatever you're comfortable with. Being in a throuple doesn't have a set of rules. Some take turns when it comes to lovemaking, others prefer a threesome in the bedroom."

"What do you want?" she asked.

"For now, a morning snuggle."

Did snuggle mean sex?

He must have deciphered her expression because he uttered a low husky chuckle. "I just mean cuddle, unless you're in the mood for something more."

"I don't know what I want," her honest admission. "I mean this is unexpected, and I don't know what I want or think."

He smiled. "Would it help if I said we've never done this before? Never wanted to?"

"Then why me?"

"Like I said, there's something about you that draws us both. Call it fate. Love at first sight—"

"Love?" she squeaked.

His eyes crinkled at the corners. "Yeah, I can't believe I said it either."

"It's too soon."

"Is it? I always wondered what people meant when they said love at first sight. In my case, it might have been the first bite of that sandwich."

"I do make a mean sandwich," she said with a lilt of her lips.

"You also wield a mean bat."

"I am sorry about that."

"Don't be. I like that you're tough. Now come here and let me enjoy your softer side." He reached for Adeline, and she scooted over to be in his arms. Nice, a different nice than Ambrose. Not better, not worse. Just different.

She pressed her cheek to his chest and could feel the steady beat of his heart.

Orion continued to talk. "I know I joked about the sandwich, but the truth is the moment I saw you, something clicked inside me."

"The moment I saw you, I thought you were a flirt."

He laughed. "I've been known to be a bit of a ladies man."

"Ambrose isn't," she stated.

"He is not. Hence his surprise at my interest in you. But there comes a time in a man's life when he finally realizes he's found what he's always been searching for."

"Me."

"Yes, you. And I'm really hoping you'll give us a chance."

Because what they suggested would be life-altering—and possibly heart-shattering—she had to ask, "Let's say I agreed to be with you both, how do I know you won't get bored and ditch me?"

"For one, Ambrose isn't the type. As for me, I told you, it's different with you. Had I wanted to just bang you, I would have done it the first time I saw you."

She snorted. "You're assuming my panties drop that easily."

"Oh, I know they don't. You're a good girl," he murmured against the top of her head.

"Not always," she retorted.

"Agreed. You were naughty last night. You enjoyed Ambrose's lovemaking."

She froze in his arms.

"It's okay. I'm not jealous. It arouses me to know you were being pleasured. Touched."

"Oh." She had no reply.

"Are you wet right now?" he whispered.

To her embarrassment, she was. She nodded.

"May I touch you?" The playboy asking for permission.

How could she refuse? "Yes."

His hand slid between her legs, parting her lips, stroking her. "Mmm. I'll bet you taste like honey."

Wait, was he going to go down on her too?

His hand kept touching. Teasing...

"What do you like?" he asked.

"What you're doing," she admitted.

"And what about when Ambrose licked you?"

She shivered. "I really liked that too."

"Do you want me to lick you?"

"Yes." She sighed the word.

He lay on his back. "Bring me that sweet pussy of yours."

"What?"

"I want you to control how I eat you, so sit that sweet pussy of yours on my face."

Her cheeks burned. "But I might hurt you."

"Oh, sweetheart, you ain't gonna hurt me unless my aching balls count."

While her cheeks might be hot, she couldn't deny

the allure of his words or suggestion. She moved so that she straddled his chest. Ambrose's shirt hung down, hiding her body from view.

"Closer," he whispered, his hands cupping her ass.

He drew her to his mouth, and she gasped as he put his lips on her. He didn't stop with just a kiss. She gripped the headboard as he tongued her thoroughly, lapping at her clit, teasing apart her lips, making her pant with need.

When he finally thrust a finger inside, she came. Hard and fast, slumping for a second before throwing herself off his face to huff, "Are you okay?"

He chuckled. "I am fantastic, sweetheart."

She eyed the tent in the blankets. "Do you need a hand?"

"Only if you want to."

She did actually. She started by creeping her hand under the covers to grab him. Thick and long. She stroked him slowly, and he closed his eyes with a groan.

Given his obvious enjoyment, she flipped back the covers and saw him, fully erect with a bit of a curve. She kept stroking him up and down and somehow missed the door opening. She froze at the sight of Ambrose standing there.

Should she apologize? Stop?

His expression smoldered as he murmured. "Keep going."

She stared at Ambrose as she stroked Orion. The

moment oddly intimate. His titillation evident by the erection pushing at his pants.

She glanced down at her right hand on Orion's cock before holding out her left to Ambrose.

His brows rose, and he mouthed, *Are you sure?*

She nodded. It didn't seem fair to give to one and not the other.

Ambrose came to the side of the bed and pushed his pants down, revealing a thicker, if shorter cock. Just as tempting. She grabbed hold and began stroking him in rhythm with Orion.

It was a surreal moment, something out of a porn flick, but she was the sexy star. She stroked them faster, bouncing in time with her motion.

To her surprise, they came at the same time, buttering her from two directions.

And what did she do?

Giggled. Because what else could a woman covered in cum do?

"I think I need a shower."

She didn't go alone. A good thing it was big enough for three.

There was much soaping going on as she tried to wash the guys while they both washed her.

It might have led to something more if Smudge didn't appear and suddenly meow at them.

Trouble had found them already.

CHAPTER 13

Ambrose would have loved to spend more time exploring the new sensual delight discovered with Adeline. He'd worried he'd be bothered by seeing her with Orion, but that fear had been assuaged the moment he'd walked in on them.

Seeing her intent on stroking Orion's cock lifted his own. And when she beckoned? He couldn't put his dick in her hand fast enough.

To his wonder, pleasuring them both excited her. Excited them all. Their slippery shower fun would have probably finished in bed if not for the cat letting out a warning yowl.

They dressed quickly. Well, he and Orion did, Adeline had a problem with garments, given they'd fled her place with none. While Orion skipped downstairs to check on the entrances, Ambrose cobbled together an outfit—large sweatshirt, track pants cinched tight, and oversized sandals since they didn't have shoes that fit and hers remained gore-covered.

As they hit the main floor, Orion, who'd gone before them, greeted them with a grim expression. "We've got company."

"How many?" Ambrose asked.

"Looks like a handful of cryptids at the front of the house, more creeping at the back."

"How did they find us?" Ambrose exclaimed. "I thought you weren't followed."

"I wasn't. And be warned, these guys are in rough shape," Orion stated.

"Rough how?" Ambrose found his choice of words odd.

"Let's just say the condition the wererat had appears more advanced."

Adeline glanced between them. "Can someone explain what that means?"

Ambrose and Orion exchanged a glance before Ambrose said, "The wererat that attacked you was technically dead."

"As in a zombie?" she squeaked.

"Yes and no. Usually a zombie is dead first then revived. These... These appear to have had their souls stripped from them while alive, and without it, the body is dead without being dead, which I know doesn't make much sense."

"What can steal a person's soul?" she asked, her brow furrowed.

"A few cryptids actually, but none that should be wandering loose about a city," Ambrose stated.

"But I'll bet the men in the black vans know." Orion pursed his lips. "We're going to need to bust out of here. This house wasn't meant to act as a fortress."

They'd be sitting ducks if they stayed. Ambrose jangled his keys. "Everyone into the SUV, and once the garage door opens, we'll make a run for it."

A pale-faced Adeline didn't say much, but she did follow orders and waited by the kitchen door with her cats standing sentinel on either side. Orion and Ambrose gathered a few key things. Mainly cash, a few weapons, and their phones. Everything else could be purchased.

Once in the garage, they could hear the approaching monsters. They moaned. Not for brains or anything so cliché. Nope, the few mumbled words they could understand, most likely from the trio of human-looking shamblers, was "Need it. So empty."

It hit Ambrose in a sudden flash of understanding. "They want their souls!"

"Makes sense, I guess, but why would they think Adeline has them?" Orion asked the most obvious question.

Adeline shrugged when they turned their glances on her. "Don't ask me. I'm human. Tested and certified." A common thing many did to see if they had any latent cryptid genetics.

"We can figure it out later. Let's head out." Ambrose led the way.

Ambrose and Orion took the front seats while Adeline crawled in the back with her cats. Their hackles were raised, but they didn't growl. However, judging by the green glow of their eyes, they readied to shift. Hopefully not in the SUV or it would get cramped.

The garage door opened, and immediately Ambrose saw a hobgoblin trying to crawl through the bottom. The more the door opened, the more bodies that clustered—some humanoid, more definitely cryptid—pushing into the space.

"I thought you said a handful," he murmured to Orion.

"Apparently, more arrived when I stopped looking."

"Hold on," Ambrose advised as he hit the gas and slammed the vehicle into reverse.

Thunk. Thud.

He kept his lips tight as he mowed down those trying to get at them. They cleared the driveway, and as Ambrose shifted into Drive, he glanced to see the bodies lying where he'd hit them, still trying to move, crawling disjointedly after them. Disturbing, to say the least.

As the SUV sped from the rental, he noticed a vehicle turning onto the street, the early dawn hour making them too visible. Could be someone passing through, though unlikely. Not taking chances, he hit the gas hard, taking the first turn he saw then another, zigzagging away in the hopes of losing any pursuers.

In the rearview mirror, he could see Adeline tight-lipped but calm. Her cats sat on the back of the seat and stared out the back window. If he were to gauge by their vigilante stance, they had a follower.

"We need to ditch the car," he stated.

"We'll be slower on foot," Orion remarked, drumming his fingers on the dash.

"I'm aware. We'll need a spot to hide."

To his surprise, Adeline piped in. "I know a place. Park here and I'll take you."

Rather than question, he trusted the woman who knew this city better than him. They parked and piled out, an odd-looking group for sure, but thankfully not many folks were out and about at this hour. Adeline took off at a brisk walk, turning immediately into an alley that stunk of garbage. She kept her brisk pace as they emerged onto a street, which she crossed to head into another alley. The cats took point, trotting ahead.

"Where are you taking us?" Orion asked, his head constantly swiveling to look in all directions.

"A place few dare to go," she murmured. "So when we get there, let me do the talking."

They emerged from an alley to a four-lane road that had an access ramp to get onto the bridge. Adeline headed for the spot underneath.

Ambrose smelled the troll well before reaching it and stopped. "Um, Adeline, you might not want to get any closer."

"Don't worry. Frank won't hurt me."

"Who's Frank?" a suspicious Orion asked.

"The troll who lives under the bridge. He won't hurt me," she repeated.

"What about the rest of us?" Orion asked.

She turned to smile and say, "Like I said, let me do the talking." She then glanced at her pets. "You might want to stay out of sight. He likes to eat cats as a snack."

The male feline hissed and arched its back, but the female kept sauntering.

The space under the bridge smelled even worse up close and showed signs of the troll having been here quite some time. A huge mound of rubbish met them —AKA the remains of what it consumed: bones, clothes, a bicycle. Cities tended to leave trolls be so long as they didn't actively hunt, but anyone foolish enough to go near... Well, that was Darwinism in action. Kids were taught young to stay away from bridge trolls.

Ambrose finally understood how Adeline used to handle her problem of unwelcome visitors. Brilliant really. The troll took care of the bodies and evidence. Some might have said her actions were cold, but he admired her resourcefulness. That quality would come in handy when she accepted them as their mate.

Yes, mate. While he and Orion might not be natural-born shifters, they had many of their traits, including the mating instinct. Not something he'd thought applicable to them before but, then again, they'd never met *the one*.

As they neared a ramshackle structure built of

metal siding, wooden pallets, and even the carcasses of a few cars, Adeline halted and yelled, "Hey, Frank. You in there?"

Thump. Thump. A massive head peered past the tarp hanging over a doorway. A few oily strands of hair sprang from the flat-topped pate. A bulbous nose, riddled with red veins, sniffed and fat lips smacked.

"Did you bring me yummies?"

"Not this time, I'm afraid. I need a favor."

The troll pondered her request, its large face squinching. "What kind of favor?"

"Me and my friends need a place to lie low until some bad guys chasing us go away."

"Will they chase you here?" the troll asked slowly.

"Probably," Orion replied a second before Ambrose could cuff him.

The troll grinned, showing off massive, yellow teeth. "Oh good. I'm hungry. Come in. Come in."

While they entered, the cats remained outside, roaming the area, sniffing. Ambrose might have liked to stay with them—because most people didn't intentionally set foot in a troll's abode—but Adeline had already entered the den.

The inside fared better than the exterior with the floor clear of debris or piles of trash. A table had been built using barrels with pallets set on top. A bed on the far wall used a half-dozen discarded mattresses and a mess of blankets. From the rafters hung sacks that Ambrose might have ignored but for the fact one of them moved.

None of his business. Trolls had to eat, and while people might not like their diet, it was in their nature to be carnivores.

"Who is chasing you?" Frank queried as he reached up into the rafters to pull down some human-sized chairs. A troll who sometimes entertained people. How unexpected.

"A bunch of folks. Soldier types in combat gear—"

"Oooh, crunchy."

"—as well as the undead."

"Seasoned meat. Even better," Frank exclaimed, clapping his hands.

Most people would have flinched or run screaming at his morbid glee, but Adeline beamed. "I knew I could trust you to help."

"I protect my friends, and you're one of them," rumbled the big fella.

Orion sidled close. "She's magnificent."

The comment almost made Ambrose snort, even as he agreed. Not many people would befriend a troll. It led to him asking, "How did you and Adeline meet?"

She replied first. "My first time disposing of an intruder, I rented a car and drove to the bridge because I know it's usually quiet."

"I don't like noisy neighbors," Frank interjected.

"Frank saw me trying to haul the body from the trunk and offered to help."

"Never waste meat!" Frank declared with a smile.

"Since then, he's been handling the intruders for me, and I pop in for a chat now and then."

"She brings nice snacks. Although I keep telling her she shouldn't cook the meat and I don't need the bread." Frank made a face.

"You come for chats?" Ambrose thought Orion might faint.

"Turns out, Frank's quite the historian," Adeline announced. "I've learned quite a bit from him."

"Been here since the bridge was just a wooden thing that I used to take tolls from. But then they put in a metal one and told me if I busted it, I'd be sent to the farm." The farm being a place for cryptids that couldn't function in society safely. "At least I'm allowed to eat anyone who comes by causing trouble." Which explained the lack of vagrancy and street crime in the area.

"That's because you're a good troll," Adeline crooned.

Ambrose held in a wince as Adeline patted the troll's hand as if he weren't a killing machine.

"I got a new sign. Want to see?"

The troll led Adeline to the other side of his abode, and Orion leaned close to whisper, "I don't know how long I can stay here without wanting to puke." The smell really overwhelmed.

"Where else can we go? Until we figure out why those soulless things are chasing her, we won't be able to stop them from tracking her down. They did it in less than twelve hours."

"I'm aware," Orion groused. "We should have taken her farther."

"Run away? Great plan, until they catch up."

"I realize it's not the best option, which is why we're here and not at an airport."

"That receipt we found, the one for the store in the industrial area... I think one of us needs to check it out," Ambrose suggested.

"Rock, paper, scissors?" Orion asked.

"Sure." Ambrose grinned as he won three out of five.

"Try not to get eaten," Ambrose said, slapping Orion on the back. He headed for Adeline. "Listen, sweetheart. I'm going to pop out for a bit and do some reconnaissance. Think you'll be okay?"

"I'll protect her." Frank thumped his chest.

"Orion's staying too. I'll be back soon as I can." Then, because she looked adorable chewing her lower lip, he dragged her close for a kiss, which led to Frank gagging.

"Ugh. Mushy."

Ambrose left, but he didn't go alone. The male cat stayed by his side, tail high.

He glanced down at it. "Ready to go find out where the bad guys are lairing?"

The eyes flashed green for a second.

He'd take that as a yes.

They quickly exited the bridge area for a street with some traffic. He debated returning to the ditched SUV. It would make travel easier, except when he retraced their steps, he saw it being hooked to a tow truck, which he might have handled but for the blacked-out van parked behind.

"Guess we're grabbing a taxi," he murmured. Good thing for his credit card. Untraceable he might add. Hekate always kept them well-supplied and anonymous.

Once in the cab, with the driver eyeing askance the cat in his backseat, Ambrose gave the directions to the corner store on the receipt they'd found.

It turned out to be a generic-type store, but in a stroke of luck, the clerk, when casually questioned, remembered seeing men in combat gear.

"Any idea where they're working out of?" Ambrose asked as he paid for some beef jerky and a drink.

"Must be close by, seeing as how they've come in a few times a day since Tuesday." Tuesday being the day the wererat got taken from CA custody.

"I wonder what they're doing in town." Ambrose played the part of curious bystander.

"Fucking feds. Probably hiding aliens or something in one of the warehouses."

Which one, though?

Ambrose took a stroll upon leaving the store, handing pieces of jerky to the cat who trotted by his side, until they reached an intersection. Straight ahead, an industrial area, but the kitty turned left.

"Where are you going?"

The cat didn't deign to reply but did flick its tail.

"Follow you, eh?" Might as well. They walked into an area that appeared more neglected, with weeds growing up through cracked pavement, the road empty of any traffic.

The attack came out of nowhere. And it wasn't really an attack. Suddenly the cat arched its back and hissed, bolting only a second before a dart smacked the spot it had been standing.

Ambrose, however, didn't prove as lucky. He got hit by rooftop snipers—one, two, three—non-magical darts that immediately turned his blood sluggish.

As he hit the ground, he could only think, *Oh shit*. Because knowing Orion, when Ambrose didn't return, he'd come looking and walk right into a trap.

CHAPTER 14

As hours passed with no word from Ambrose, Adeline worried.

When Frank went to check on a noise outside his home, she couldn't help but express it. "Shouldn't Ambrose have been back by now?"

Orion, in a rare moment of seriousness, nodded. "We should have heard from him. I've tried texting, but his phone is offline."

"Do you think he got caught?"

"He's pretty tricky." Orion tried to reassure, but she could see his concern.

"Maybe we should go looking for him."

"Not we. If Ambrose got snagged, then the last thing we need is for them to catch you, too."

"This is such a mess," she huffed, pacing the floor. "I mean, why are zombies coming after me? Do I have like a super-yummy brain they can't resist?"

"I'd have said more like you have an irresistible peach."

She pursed her lips. "Not the time."

"I know, but I hate seeing you worried."

"Can't you ask your goddess?"

"I have." His lips turned down. "She isn't answering." He hastened to add, "Hekate's weird about replying to prayers. Sometimes, she's quick. Other times, it might be days or even weeks before she talks to us."

"Do you like serving her?"

"She saved my life. Mine and Ambrose's. We were on a path that would have seen us dead before we became men. In our time, orphans didn't have many options but petty theft or whoring."

"How old are you?"

"Old enough." He winked.

Frank stomped back in. "No crunchies yet." He sounded put out.

"I can't stand this waiting anymore," Adeline declared. Ambrose went into danger for her. If he needed rescuing, she couldn't sit around.

"What are you doing?" Orion asked as she headed for the tarp over the doorway.

"Going to find Ambrose."

"But you don't know where he is."

"You do, though," she riposted.

Orion sighed. "If I go looking, will you promise to stay here with Frank?"

"What if you get caught?"

"Then I guess you, Frank, and the cats will have to save me."

"Deal." A promise made with no idea how she'd do it. She'd figure it out when and if needed.

"Kiss for good luck?" he asked.

She grabbed him by the shirt and smooched him hard, and Frank coughed.

"Stop," Frank rumbled.

"Sorry. I forgot you hate mushy stuff," she laughed a tad breathlessly.

Frank shook his head. "No time for it. I smell visitors."

Her eyes widened. "They're here!"

While she trembled in sudden fear, Frank's face split into a smile of happiness. "Yummies in my tummy!" He grabbed a club, a tree trunk with nails jutting from the tip. He thrust it over his shoulder and went to stand by the door.

Adeline wrung her hands, feeling useless without her taser or bat.

Orion pressed something cold and metallic into her hand. She glanced down to see a dagger.

"Why are you giving me this?"

"Because my paws can't hold it. Don't be afraid to use it," he advised as he stripped.

If she'd not been trembling with fear, she might have drooled over his fine physique.

"You're going to shift, aren't you?" she asked as he placed his clothes on the table.

"Yup." He cupped her head and dragged her in for a kiss and a whisper. "Be safe, sweetheart."

"How about you don't die," she replied, trying to not give in to panic.

"Bah, I'm too pretty to die under a bridge." He winked and, in the blink of an eye, went from six-foot hunk to big sleek-furred dog.

With a bark, he bounded off, popping through the tarp without hesitation.

Frank glanced at her. "He better not eat my yummies."

She laughed only so as not to cry.

This was happening.

Holy scary.

Frank went charging without warning, club raised, ready to fight, whereas Adeline crept to the doorway and peered out, her view somewhat blocked by the mound of trash. Movement startled her until she realized it was Smudge.

"Where's Fudge?" she asked, her cat rarely without her brother.

Smudge meowed and shrugged. More answer than she'd expected.

"How many are they fighting?"

She could hear Frank yodeling. "Ooh, crunchy and chunky." *Thunk*. "Never had hobgoblin before." *Thud*. The latter impact came flying toward her and landed in a tangled heap of bent limbs.

The hobgoblin, despite being broken with bones jutting, managed to twist its head, and its mouth soundlessly opened and shut in her direction. It should have been dead.

Only one way to kill a zombie.

She strode over, took a deep breath, and shoved the dagger down through its cranium. It proved easier than expected. She pulled the blade free and grimaced at the slime on it.

She couldn't afford to be squeamish, though. *I should be helping.* After all, the attack occurred because of her. She tightened her grip on the dagger, marched past the debris, and halted at the sight of the battle.

Orion ran through shambling bodies, taking them out by the ankles. Those that kept heading for the shack—AKA Adeline—got in Frank's reach where he whacked them with his studded club. One smack and they didn't stand back up. But the number on the ground was nothing compared to those still moving. She counted a good two dozen, and as if under one hive mind, they all faced her.

Making sure to steer clear of Frank's swing, she entered the battle, going after the ones who crawled as the easiest targets.

Some looked monstrous and were easy to dagger. Others had faces. One, a girl with silvery skin, couldn't have been more than a teen. Adeline also noticed that those in clothing all wore essentially the same outfit. Come to think of it, the ones at the rental had as well. Scrub bottoms and tops, the gray of them filthy. Had they escaped from a hospital?

As the zombies died—for the second time—she

almost grinned. *We did it*. A preemptive victory, given Orion's sudden furious barking.

She glanced past him to see—

"Crunchy dinner!" Frank yelled, charging for the soldiers in combat gear who came trotting into view.

Boom. Boom. Each step of the troll reverberated, but the men in black didn't flee. They knelt and took aim.

"Frank, no!. Be careful!" she screamed as they fired.

Frank halted in his tracks, his body jerking as projectiles hit him. He teetered on his feet, and it wasn't until someone yelled, "He's going down," that it occurred to her to get out of the way or she'd get crushed.

She darted to the side, the one opposite Orion. Smudge joined her, the cat mega-sized once more, whiskers messy from helping.

Kaboom.

Frank hit the ground like a bomb.

As the tremor subsided, Adeline blinked. Poor Frank. He didn't deserve to die like that.

Snore.

The noisy inhalation and exhalation had her sagging with relief. Not dead, just asleep.

The soldiers were shooting tranquilizers. The second she thought it, they hit Orion. Not that one dart took him down. He snarled and lunged for the closest guy with a gun, but as he wrestled it from the marksman's hands, another shot him. And another.

Poor Orion howled as he slumped, a sound that tapered into silence and left Adeline standing alone.

Not good. How about terrifying?

One of the men approached her. "You need to come with us."

She shook her head and exclaimed, "What are you doing with Orion?" Four soldiers had grabbed and lifted him.

"Taking him to the same place you're going. Don't make us do this the hard way," the man cajoled, holding out a gloved hand.

"Who are you? Why do you want me?"

"Ma'am, this doesn't have to be difficult."

"Difficult?" she shrieked. "You sent zombies after me. You tranqued my friends."

"Someone knock her out." The man tossed the order over his shoulder, and she clenched her fists, rage filling her, hot and furious.

"Holy shit. Why is she glowing?" someone exclaimed.

Who, her?

"Shoot her now!" screamed the man a second before a car suddenly came plummeting from the bridge, striking him dead-on.

She gaped.

Everyone did.

Then chaos erupted. A soldier went to fire and mega-Smudge leaped, knocking the muzzle aside, saving Adeline from the dart. The rifleman swung the butt of his gun and struck her kitty.

My baby! How dare they.

The van parked closest to the group suddenly had flames shooting from under the hood. Men scrambled, one heading for cover by the trash heap, which suddenly toppled, burying him. Another close to the river's edge screamed as suddenly the ground crumbled, dumping him into the water. Another vehicle came crashing down from the bridge, squishing two more soldiers.

That was the point where all of them scattered.

The van holding Orion took off with spinning tires, and she could only helplessly watch.

Soon there was just her, Smudge, and a snoring Frank.

The battle was over. She remained free, but Orion and Ambrose...

Frank suddenly stirred and stretched. "That was a nice nap. What happened to the crunchies?"

"They're gone," her dull reply.

"Bummer," Frank muttered.

"I have to go." She couldn't stay there, and so, with Smudge in tow, she went to the one place that had been her haven for almost two decades.

The sandwich shop.

CHAPTER 15

AMBROSE WOKE IN A CAGE. NOT HIS FIRST TIME, ACTUALLY. People had a tendency to cage dogs. But this time he'd been placed in one as a man. A man who'd foolishly been ambushed. In his defense, he hadn't expected snipers in the city. At least they'd been using sleeping darts and not bullets. Healing from holes hurt, especially when Hekate didn't answer her prayers promptly.

His clothes had been removed and replaced with gray scrubs. His feet remained bare. Phone and wallet gone. Not that either would do his captors any good. His identification had a false name and an address he never used. His cell had a password lock that would reset the device after two failed attempts.

The hard floor of his cell didn't have a mattress pad or even a blanket to cut the harsh cement surface. A smelly bucket in a corner made him grimace. Hopefully he wouldn't have to use it.

As he rose, he stretched and looked around. Then looked again in disbelief. The massive space didn't have any windows, but the fluorescent lighting overhead provided harsh clarity. It Concrete built with pillars rising to a ceiling about twenty feet overhead. Cages filled the area for the most part, although he did see a row of glass tanks along a back wall, the fluid in them varying, from clear water to murky.

The tanks held creatures, at least the ones he could see. A kraken, slightly larger than the one they'd fought, drifted listlessly along the bottom of one. In one of the cloudy tanks, a sudden webbed hand slapped against the glass. Disturbing but not as disturbing as the people and cryptids he could see in the cells like his. Some of the captives huddled in corners or hunched in the middle, holding their knees, rocking, many audibly sobbing. Others gripped the bars, pleading for mercy or screaming to be set free.

The scarier ones? Those with blank faces who just stood, staring vacantly while mumbling. He had a feeling he knew what happened to them.

They've lost their souls.

And lucky him, he might be next.

Fuck. As he took in more details, he noted they wore the same scrubs as him, the state of them appearing to vary depending on their length of stay. Those who showed emotion remained fairly clean-looking. The zombie types? Filthy and uncaring.

What was this place? How could it be the Cryptid Authority didn't know of this many people being taken captive? Or did they know? He couldn't help but recall that the unidentified soldiers just marched into a CA office and took the wererat. It made sense, they'd been taking back into custody one of their escaped patients. Whoever ran this outfit would hardly want news of their experiments getting out, because this was an experiment. Of that, he had no doubt.

Oh, Hekate, what have you gotten us embroiled in this time? And what did it have to do with Adeline?

Of more worry, the way he couldn't touch his goddess. Praying usually gave him a certain feeling, that even if not heard he knew she'd received. But praying right now just seemed to disappear into a void, the shielding on this place somehow god-proof.

Not good.

A commotion drew his attention, and he saw the combat-geared men entering, pushing a gurney, upon which lay a black hound. His blood chilled at the realization they'd captured Orion. In better news, he didn't see Adeline. Had she evaded the soldiers? Or...

He refused to even contemplate a worse scenario. No way had she died.

The soldiers dumped Orion into the empty cage across from him and left without saying a word. Ambrose didn't even bother trying to engage them in conversation because he doubted they'd say anything.

The moment the room cleared of soldiers, he gripped the bars and hissed, "Orion. Wake up. Now's not the time to be napping."

His friend continued to snore softly. They must have doped him good. It would eventually wear off. In the meantime, he needed to find a way out. He inspected the cage, running his hands over the bars and the welds holding them in place. Trailing his fingers over the lock on the door zapped him.

"You can't escape." The soft whisper came from his left.

Ambrose turned to see a cyclops, one of the calmer prisoners, sitting cross-legged in his prison. "What is this place?"

"Hell?" The cyclops shrugged. "I don't know. One minute, I was minding my business, tending my garden, the next I woke here."

"Have you seen anyone other than the soldiers?"

"Nope. And they don't stay long. Either they're bringing someone new or taking someone out. Although I think something big must be happening because they removed most of the lobotomized prisoners at the morning meal."

"Lobotomized?" Ambrose queried.

"Don't know what else to call it. People leave here yelling and fighting, they come back zoned out." The cyclops ducked his head as he murmured, "It will be my turn soon. I've been here longest."

"All the more reason to escape."

"How? These locks can't be picked. The bars can't be bent."

"What about when the soldiers open the doors?"

"One against the half-dozen they send?" The cyclops pointed out the bad odds.

"Half-dozen? Bah." Ambrose had faced worse and prevailed.

"I wish you luck, friend." The cyclops stiffened as they heard the main entrance to the room opening, the electronic whir of the mechanism to roll the door drawing attention.

A group of soldiers entered, one pushing a gurney, which they wheeled to the cyclops' cage.

Despite having mentioned the futility, the cyclops tried to fight. Rushing the soldier who opened his prison, swinging a big ham-sized fist then grappling with the half-dozen who waited.

The cyclops lost, as they zapped him from multiple directions with a cattle prod. Once they'd subdued the cyclops, they heaved him onto the gurney and strapped him tight. As it rolled by, he turned his head and whispered, "Goodbye and good luck."

With the cyclops' departure, the room grew quiet, a somber mood falling over those who still had their awareness. It lasted until the soldiers returned with the cyclops. They dumped him into his cage and left.

"Hey, friend, are you okay?" Ambrose tried speaking to him, but the cyclops stood in his cell staring at nothing. It led to Ambrose shouting, "Snap out of it. What happened?"

The head swiveled slowly, and the cyclops' words emerged even slower. "I am empty. They took it."

Took his soul.

It frightened Ambrose like nothing he'd ever faced before.

"What the fuck? Where am I?" Orion groaned as he roused from his drugged sleep.

"You're in a shit-ton of trouble. We both are," Ambrose stiffly replied.

Orion stood and stretched, his naked body rippling. "Fuck me. Where's Adeline?"

"You tell me. I take it you were attacked after I left."

"Zombies then soldiers armed with tranqs. I got knocked out during the fight. Last I saw, Adeline was fighting."

"Maybe Frank got her to safety?"

Orion's lips turned down. "Frank got taken down before me."

"Fuck." Ambrose swore softly.

"Yeah. So what is place?"

"We appear to be where they're making the soulless." Ambrose waved a hand. "Behold the before and after."

"We need to get out of here." Orion repeated Ambrose's earlier statement.

"Agreed, but short of you having a lock pick or a hacksaw up your ass, we're kind of stuck."

"They've got to open this cage eventually." Orion grabbed the bars and pulled uselessly at them.

"And when they do, we fight." Ambrose's lips flattened. "It would help if I could speak to the goddess. Can you contact her?"

Orion frowned. "No. It's like I'm in a dead zone. I feel nothing."

"Same." Ambrose didn't like it one bit. While he didn't regularly chat with Hekate, for decades now, he'd felt the warmth of her blessing. A warmth that was now gone.

Whir. Click.

The main door opened again, and more than a half-dozen soldiers emerged, the pair in the lead holding cattle prods, while the last of the group pushed a gurney.

As they neared Ambrose's cage, he backed away. He had no interest in getting zapped.

A short, stocky soldier barked, "No trouble from you or you'll regret it." To emphasize the threat, one of the zappers made his prod crackle.

"Where are you taking me?" Ambrose asked as they opened his cage.

"You'll soon see. Get on the bed." The stocky man pointed.

Ambrose pretended compliance and walked with a measured pace. Three strides and he exited the cage. But rather than lie down, he lunged to his left, grabbing the cattle prod and yanking it free. The second one jabbed him in the back and zapped.

Ambrose didn't go down, but he did yell because it fucking hurt. He swung his arms and felt his fist connect, solidly too; however, the effort turned out to be for nothing. With sheer numbers alone, they subdued him, hefting him onto the gurney and strapping him down.

Orion yelled, "Let him go! You'll regret this! We are Hekate's hounds. She won't be happy to find out you've taken us."

The soldiers didn't give a fuck. They wheeled Ambrose out of the horrifying basement into an elevator, the cab cramped with his rolling bed and their many bodies. Only half exited when the door opened, pushing his bed along a white sterile hall. He still couldn't contact Hekate, but he tried.

Goddess, I could really use a bit of help.

No reply.

A solid, steel-built door sat at the end of the hall with a security screen on either side. The chunky soldier removed his helmet and stepped to one of the screens to let it scan his face. The other required a woman in a white coat who suddenly arrived, obviously important given how fast the soldiers flattened themselves to the wall so she could pass through.

She let the screen scan an access card, and only then did the door open.

"I've got him from here," she stated, grabbing his bed and pushing it into the room, which turned out to be full of lab equipment.

"Who are you?" Ambrose asked.

She pretended as if he'd not spoken as she parked him in front of another door that required scanning. Then she wheeled him into the next chamber, a room with padding all over and an even more dulling sensation compared to the basement.

What had they done to this place to make it god-proof?

"Rise and shine, Thaddeus. I've got another one for you."

Only when she spoke did Ambrose realize the room held someone else. A man, rather large in size but not fat, just very tall and broad-shouldered with a military-style crew cut. He sat in a chair in a corner, and at her words, he rose. Another prisoner, but why keep him apart?

And why did he seem familiar? Ambrose would have sworn he'd never seen the man before.

"Must I?" the man murmured. "This will be the fifth today."

"We need this one. He's got a connection to our target. We can use that to hopefully snare her."

Ambrose wanted to fist pump. Adeline hadn't been caught!

"No more after this one. I need to recover," muttered the man.

"No whining. Get this done while I make a call." The woman exited, and the man named Thaddeus neared Ambrose. While Ambrose detected nothing unusual about him, a bad feeling travelled through him.

He tried reasoning. "Whatever it is she wants you to do, you don't have to. Set me free and I can help you."

"There is no help for me. Just pain. Pain and loneliness." Thaddeus' lips turned down. "I am sorry. This won't take long."

The man held out his hand. He didn't even touch Ambrose, and yet fear filled him, and he prayed one last time, *Goddess, save me.*

CHAPTER 16

The sandwich shop mocked Adeline with its closed sign. Her own fault, given she'd not shown up to work or given anyone notice. In her defense, she'd been a tad busy—and not just fooling around with two sexy studs. Running for her life meant she'd fled with nothing, including her keys. She could have gone to her apartment to see if she could grab them unnoticed, but she lacked the energy. Not to mention it might still be watched. Heck, her shop might not be safe. She glanced around suspiciously. Saw nothing, but would she notice?

Some might wonder why she'd gone to her place of work, which her pursuers most likely knew about. However, by her logic, most people would avoid their job in a crisis, hence it made it the least likely place to find her—and a waste of time since she couldn't get inside.

Now what? She stared forlornly at the shop.

To her surprise, the lock clicked. She opened the door to see Keeble standing there. "You're late," he accused. "Your morning tea is cold."

"I'm sorry," she mumbled. "It was a rough night."

His eyes widened as he took in her appearance. "What happened to you?"

She entered and locked the door, leaving the sign flipped to close. She slumped onto her stool behind the counter before answering Keeble. "Where should I start? I had to deal with a kraken last night that came up through my tub. Its guts are currently plastered all over my apartment. As if that weren't enough, I'm hiding from zombies and secret soldiers. And before you ask, I don't know why they're after me."

"Uh-oh," Keeble muttered. "The boss won't like this."

She glanced at him. "It's not like I did it on purpose."

"No. Of course not. Let me get you some tea." Before he could scamper off, she huffed, "I don't want tea." She wanted her quiet normal life back. She wanted to not be attacked. She wanted Ambrose and Orion safe.

As her emotions bubbled, a car across the street crashed into a hydrant.

Keeble pinched his lips, observing the wreck before asserting, "You definitely need some tea."

No point in arguing. She leaned her face in her hands and gave in to a bit of self-pity. *Woe is me.* From best night with two hotties to on the run and alone.

A nudge at her leg had her peeking down to see Smudge leaning against her. "Hey, baby. I'll bet you're worried about Fudge." Given he'd not been around for the battle, she could only assume he'd either left her for greener pastures or accompanied Ambrose.

Keeble emerged from the back with the steaming mug.

She took it from him and had a nice long sip.

Aaah. The relaxation hit instantly and disappeared almost as fast when Keeble ruined it by announcing, "The boss is coming to see you."

"Great because all this day needs to finish it off is for me to be fired in person." She sighed. How had her quiet existence turned into this chaos?

"He's here," Keeble declared.

She startled. "That was quick."

"The boss doesn't travel the usual ways." A comment that led to her frowning, but before she could ask what he meant, Keeble fled, saying, "I'll let you two talk."

The shop darkened as if all the lights went out, and yet she could see them still lit, faint spots amidst an encroaching gloom. The wisps of shadow coalesced into a tall shape, possibly a man, but hard to tell given the voluminous flowing cloak, a swath of fabric that undulated as if tugged by an invisible breeze.

The entity loomed over her, an ominous presence that left her mouth dry.

"Hello, Adeline." The deep voice sent a shiver through her.

"Hi," she rasped. Could this be the mysterious Mr. Charyx? "Are you my boss?"

"Among other things," a reply that emerged from the cowl of the cloak.

"I guess you're here to fire me for not showing up this morning." Her lips turned down. "If it helps, circumstances made it impossible for me to be here for opening." Would it be whining if she told him her troubles to try and save her job?

"You're not being fired."

"Then why are you here?" Because she'd never once seen her boss in person. Even now it almost felt as if he weren't completely there. Was he doing some kind of astral projection?

"I am here because it would appear current events require some explanation and intervention."

"Wait, you know what's going on with the zombies and soldiers?" She eyed her boss, his hood so deep she couldn't see a thing. Was he even human under there? Most likely not.

"Yes, I'm aware of everything. The saga that brought us to this moment began more than forty years ago."

"Which is before I was born, so not sure what it has to do with anything."

"Do you mind not interrupting? I am trying to explain," Mr. Charyx snapped tersely.

"Sorry. Go ahead." Adeline remained slumped, wondering what her boss's life story had to do with anything.

"It had been several centuries since my last sabbatical on Earth."

"Centuries?" Her brows arched. "Guess that confirms you're not human." She'd kind of already figured that part out. If she didn't know better, she'd say she talked to a Grim Reaper, only those weren't real. Or at least not a recognized cryptid. She'd once spent more than an hour on a Reddit question dedicated to arguing their existence, with the consensus being they were simply a story.

"Not even close to human," was his dry reply. "Anyhow, during my sabbatical, I chose to take a corporeal form and travelled your plane for several years, visiting landmarks I'd never had a chance to explore while working, tasting the local cuisine. I also met a woman."

That piqued her interest. "So this is a love story?"

"Again, not quite. I am not capable of affection such as you mortals indulge in. However, I am capable of experiencing carnal pleasure."

Her nose wrinkled. "Ew. No offense, but I'd rather not hear about your sex life."

"Are you done interrupting?" The cloaked figure undulated in agitation.

"Excuse me for trying to have a conversation," she grumbled.

"Given Felicia's attractive nature, we made plans to meet in a more intimate setting. Alas, I did not know her flirtation was a ruse. She and her cohort, using an artifact long thought destroyed, trapped me.

Kept me prisoner as they ran tests and took samples." As his voice lowered, and deepened, his cloak rippled.

"But you escaped," Adeline remarked.

"I did. However, given their temerity, I destroyed the place that dared hold me captive and all those who participated. All except Felicia. She managed to evade me."

"Still not grasping why this is important." But it was kind of interesting.

"Despite my thoroughness in destroying their place of research, a stolen sample did survive. My semen to be exact."

She blinked. "Oh." She couldn't say much else because she suddenly began putting pieces together, and she didn't like the picture they formed.

"That semen was injected into human females, and through some feat of magic I thought impossible between our kind, gestation occurred."

"Is this where you tell me you're my daddy?" Not really a joke because she already guessed the answer.

The entity in the cloak shuddered. "Yes, I am your father. Not by choice."

"Gee, thanks. Nice to know." She paused before saying, "So you're saying my mom was artificially impregnated with me?"

"Yes, but I remained unaware of your existence until you were a young adult by your kind's measure."

"So you find out you're a daddy, but rather than meeting me face to face to say hi, you offered me a job. No offense, but that's kind of messed up." At the same time, the job had been a godsend. She'd had a streak of bad luck in her previous places of employment, many freak accidents leading to deaths. The sandwich shop provided the first place where her coworkers didn't die disturbingly often.

"I told you I am not capable of emotions."

"Says the guy who got pissed and demolished a place and the people working there," she pointed out.

The cloak went still. "That wasn't anger but self-preservation. My blood in the wrong hands could do terrible things. But my semen is even worse. There is a reason why humans and my kind aren't compatible. The offspring are dangerous."

"Me? Dangerous?" She laughed. "Boy, do you have me pegged wrong."

"You aren't consciously a threat. However, you are emotional, a trait inherited from your maternal side. Those emotions can have unexpected and dire consequences for the humans around you. Those fatalities are how I discovered your existence. Once I realized what had been done, I should have ended the experiment."

So much to take in. "I'm a science experiment?" she huffed. Then she latched onto the latter part of his statement. "You were going to kill me?"

"It's the usual course of action for one such as you, but I found myself oddly reluctant to end your life. Therefore I found a way to render you harmless to those around you."

"What do you mean, make me harmless? I was never a threat to begin with," she stated.

"Not true. I'm sure you noticed an abnormal amount of people dying around you as you grew."

For a second, she thought of what happened under the bridge and then all the other times she'd been witness to fluke accidents. Her mouth rounded. "Wait, you're saying those were my fault?"

"Not intentionally, however intense emotional events can trigger your power, and the result is people die."

"When you say power, what exactly do you mean?"

"The power to sever souls from their fleshly forms."

"Oh. Wow." She blinked. "That probably explains why those soldiers might want to get their hands on me. They see me as a potential threat, but what's the story with the zombies?"

"They are not zombies but *immortui*, thus called because they've had their souls extracted. Their bodies live, but they feel an emptiness within them, which leads to them seeking what they've lost."

"Hold on. If they're looking for their souls, why come after me?"

"Because you are *anima dissecuerit*, a sunderer and keeper of souls, thus a magnet for the *immortui*."

"If you're my father, then does that make you the Grim Reaper?" She meant it quite seriously because, despite the missing scythe, the whole flowing-robe thing made him look an awful lot like the depictions in books and movies. But grim reapers weren't supposed to be a thing.

"That is one of my titles." The weird got weirder.

"Do you have a name?" she asked.

"I am known as Charon."

"*The* Charon?" she squeaked. "I thought Charon was a ferryman who took souls across the Styx to Hell."

She'd have sworn she heard him snort. "A rumor that has persisted despite its great inaccuracy. It is my task to gather souls that enter the Styx, which some humans call limbo, and guide them not to Hell, but to a new destination for rebirth."

"Wow." Because what else was there to say? She frowned. "So me being half a grim reaper is why the soulless are after me?"

"They are after you because of the souls that cling to you rather than enter the Styx."

"Wait, are you saying I'm wearing souls right now?"

He reached for her, his sleeve falling back from a skeleton of a hand. As he pinched the fingers, for a second, she saw a glowing shape that he plucked from her. "You are covered in them currently due to recent events. I didn't have the time to remove them from your aura."

It was kind of creepy knowing she technically wore dead people. "When you say you remove them... when since we never met before?"

"When you sleep. Keeble informs me when you start accumulating a few, and I pay a visit. Alas, I'd been remiss of late due to circumstances elsewhere. The accumulation of them around you is what attracted the *immortui*. They want you to return what has been sundered."

"How can I fix them when I'm not the one who took their soul in the first place?"

"You misunderstand. They don't want the souls clustering around you. They see you as a conduit to the Styx, where they hope to reconnect with their original souls."

"Pretty sure I don't know how to get to the river of souls. I can barely manage to get around the city without getting lost."

"You and the *immortui* would die if you were to enter the Styx, as it is not meant for fleshly forms."

"So if you take the souls I have stuck to me, will these soulless freaks stop seeking me out?"

"Only temporarily, as you are a magnet for the deceased who try to avoid passing on. To cease the attacks entirely, we need to prevent the *immortui* from being created and eliminate those that exist."

"Seems cruel to kill them for something that wasn't their fault."

"It is the only option for these unnatural beings."

"Just so we're clear, I'm not the one taking their souls. Or if I am, I swear it's not on purpose." Adeline held up her hands in innocence.

"I am aware you are not the one responsible. The

tea Keeble has been giving you dulls the inadvertent use of your power."

A tea she'd only had a sip of in the last two days. "What happens if I don't drink the tea?"

Charon turned his head to eye the crashed car out front surrounded by emergency vehicles. "When your emotions become intense, accidents will happen."

It chilled her to realize how many deaths she'd caused. *I'm a murderer.* Not intentionally, and yet, all those people, all those fluke events that led to deaths... *my fault.*

"If I'm not the one making the soulless, then who?"

"You weren't the only one incubated."

"What?"

Her father, the Grim Reaper, dropped a bombshell. "You have a brother."

CHAPTER 17

Orion paced his cage, worried, a little scared, but also pissed. In all his decades of working for Hekate, he and Ambrose had been in some tough binds, but never any as bad as this one. He only had to look around the room at the zombies staring blankly off into space to realize this might finally be the adventure that brought them down. And just when he'd finally found his mate!

So unfair. He'd not even gotten to properly fuck or gotten to the part where he finally used the L word in a three-word sentence. Instead of spending time with Adeline, he was stuck in a cage, waiting to see if Ambrose came back catatonic, wondering when it would be his turn, while, at the same time, worrying about poor Adeline. He had no idea what had happened to her. Was she alive? A prisoner? In hiding?

He had no way of knowing. He couldn't even

contact his goddess. Something about this prison blocked his prayers. He'd never felt so alone.

The cage didn't provide much room for his pacing agitation, and everywhere he looked only made it worse. How could such a place exist? Did they have a necromancer of some kind creating the zombies? And why their interest in Adeline?

When the elevator whirred, he spun to watch. The doors to it opened, and only a pair of soldiers emerged accompanying Ambrose, only he wasn't Ambrose anymore.

Orion held tight to his horror as his blank-faced friend, with a stiff-legged walk, moved in the direction the soldiers pointed him.

They took his soul.

It almost made him cry. But he'd been through tough times before. He knew better than to give up.

When the soldiers left, Orion called out to Ambrose. "Hey, dude, you in there?"

No reply, not even an acknowledgement. Ambrose stood, staring vacantly ahead of him.

"I'm going to get us out of here," Orion huffed. "Hekate will fix you." And if she couldn't, she would know of someone who could, because the alternative? No, Orion wouldn't even think it. Ambrose would be okay. There was no other acceptable outcome.

Time passed, but Orion couldn't have said how long. The lighting never changed, but some soldiers did come with trolleys of food. Some kind of porridge for those who still had personalities, like Orion and the woman sobbing a few cages down. For Ambrose and the other zombies, nothing. They didn't feed them at all.

Orion tried shouting at them. "What are you doing? This is wrong, and you know it." Appealing to their moral side proved futile. People with a conscience wouldn't condone or abet the actions here.

Not long after they passed the gruel out, the elevator whirred again, sending some into a panic of sobbing and pleading. Orion almost joined them, especially since the soldiers marched to his cage, eight of them in total for him, plus one to remove a docile Ambrose.

A fellow with a high-pitched nasally voice unlocked his cage. "Let's go. You're wanted upstairs."

"By who?" Orion asked.

"No talking. Move your ass or we'll move it for you." The many cattle prods aimed in his direction made it clear they hoped he'd fight.

"I'm coming. Don't get your panties in a twist," he grumbled, stepping out of his prison.

Interesting how they'd not chosen to drag him out on a gurney. Even more interesting, they brought Ambrose as well.

The elevator ride proved entertaining with him and Ambrose in the very middle ringed by the soldiers with their cattle prods aimed and ready to zap. Orion could have probably caused trouble and even won; however, he found himself curious at the odd behavior. Something must have happened. The soldiers were tense. What had them all spinning, and could he use it to his advantage?

The floor they spilled out on had windows, lots of them that showed a purple and pink sky from the setting sun. They marched him to a boardroom with a massive wooden table flanked by a dozen leather office-type chairs, some with people seated in them.

A woman with pinched lips stood at the head of the table, her white lab coat open over a blue blouse and dark slacks. Another woman at the table, this one in military uniform, glanced at him before returning to stare at her laptop. He counted four more military types and three suits. None of them noticeably cryptid. As for their scent? Very much human.

While Orion took in everything, Ambrose suddenly came to life—so to speak. He began striding for the window, muttering, "I need it. Must get it. So empty."

Given the last time Orion heard those words happened to be in that restaurant, aimed at Adeline, his heart began to thump.

"What's he doing?" barked a grizzled fellow with a buzz cut and a few medals pinned to his chest. "I thought you said this place was shielded."

"It is," murmured the woman in the lab coat. "I can only assume the proximity of our target is too much for our precautions."

Orion listened but didn't quite understand.

The woman in charge eyed him. "You're sure these are the two subjects requested?" the woman asked.

"Yes, ma'am. Names are Orion and Ambrose.

According to our file on them, they are god-blessed humans," the military lady replied without looking up from her laptop.

"Really?" The woman eyed him intently. "They don't look that special. What magical skills do they have?"

"They can shift into dogs, Dr. Monroe." Once more the lady with the laptop had the answer.

"Dogs? Blech. We've got plenty of shifters already," the crew-cut military dude declared with disdain.

"Indeed, we do, General Benton." Dr. Monroe addressed those assembled. "Any objections to releasing them?"

"I object. The one still has all his cognition and will talk about what he's seen," the general complained.

"It will be a short-lived release. Soon as we have the target in custody, we'll take them back as well," Monroe stated.

What target did they keep yapping about? While they'd not used a name, Orion's stomach tightened because he had a feeling, given Ambrose's actions, who they spoke of.

"Why all this commotion over one person?" countered a man in a suit.

"Have you not been reading the reports?" The white-coated woman swept a hand to the window with Ambrose pressed against it mumbling. "It clearly stated that the escaped subjects sought her out. Preliminary reports indicate she is most likely the second subject that went missing from the early days of the Grim Experiment."

"She is the right age," murmured the military woman. "Although the mother's name doesn't match that of the surrogate."

"Most likely she changed it to throw us off her trail," the doctor surmised.

Surrogate? She? Pieces of the puzzle remained missing, but Orion understood enough to realize who they spoke of.

Orion exploded. "Leave Adeline alone."

"No one is talking to you," Monroe's cold reply.

"Maybe you should be because what you're doing is wrong. Taking people's souls? What kind of depraved shit is that?" he countered.

"It's called science," Monroe stated. "It's called finding ways to fight against the cryptids that are slowly infiltrating every human space in the world."

"They're not causing harm," he countered.

"Tell that to the mother whose baby got swapped by a changeling. Or the swimmer who got drowned by a selkie. The family slaughtered by a werewolf." The woman snapped out reasons, but Orion could play that game.

"What of the pixies kept in cages so folks can sell their dust? The nymphs forced into sexual slavery? The mermaids kept as novelties for the rich?"

Monroe waved a hand. "What of it? They're not human but animals."

"Animals that can talk and have feelings," Orion argued.

"Then they should have been smarter," drawled the military general. "We're in a war, humans against everything else. And we finally have a weapon to use."

What weapon? Orion would have liked to find out more, but the woman clapped her hands. "Someone gag and bind him. We don't need him spooking the target. Let's get them both to the main floor to do the exchange."

Orion wasn't about to allow himself to be bound. He spun and smashed his fist into the visor of the nearest soldier. That man staggered, but the others reacted quickly, poking him with the electrified prods, sending him to his knees, his whole body trembling, his jaw clenched.

His arms got yanked behind his back and zip tied. A wad of tissues stuffed in his mouth.

Hekate. Your hound needs your aid. He tried praying, and while he didn't get the stonewall of before, she didn't reply.

He had no choice but to be marched back into the elevator going down, Ambrose, still showing no signs of life, by his side. When the doors opened, the soldiers formed a wall at his back, pushing him and Ambrose forward, not that his friend argued. Ambrose slept-walk out into the falling twilight, whereas Orion stalked.

He had to figure out a way to protect Adeline.

Across the parking lot, he could see a slight figure

flanked by two cats. Adeline had foolishly come to trade her life for theirs. She bravely drew closer, and he could see she'd managed to get changed since he'd last seen her, the jeans and hoodie fitting her properly, the shoes on her feet a light pink.

"Here's the prisoners you asked for," declared a guy by his side.

Adeline stopped a few paces away and cocked her head. "What did you do to Ambrose?"

"He's just being quiet on account of the drugs," lied the soldier with the nasally voice.

"I'm sure he is." Adeline strode closer, standing confident though grim of expression. Her gaze flicked over him, and her lips pinched, but when she glanced at Ambrose, sorrow filled her eyes. "I'll fix this," she whispered as she passed them.

How could she fix anything if she handed herself over?

Orion craned to look over his shoulder. Ambrose turned, too, muttering, "Need it.

When Ambrose and Orion would have followed her into the building, the soldiers blocked them.

"Git. You're not needed anymore."

Orion glared. If he didn't have his hands tied...

As you wish, Hekate replied suddenly and acted too. Magic warmed his wrists and the zip ties fell to the ground. Oh hell yeah.

He yanked the tissue from his mouth and snarled, "Out of my way."

The soldiers formed a tight wall and held out their prods. "Or what?" sassed the nasally fellow.

"Or we will fuck you up!" Ambrose stated before letting his fist fly.

Rather than gape at his friend's sudden recovery, Orion joined him in giving the soldiers the beating they so richly deserved. They had help, Smudge and Fudge having expanded in size to join the fray.

It didn't take long before they had a groaning heap at their feet.

Only then did Orion eye Ambrose and say, "Are you really you?"

His friend smiled. "Yeah."

"But your soul..."

"Was never taken. Not for lack of trying. They're holding some guy prisoner and forcing him to obey, only he's tired of it. When he saw the color of my soul, which is apparently a really sparkly silver, he asked me if I served a god. When I told him I was Hekate's scion, he begged me to help him escape. I agreed, which is when we faked him taking my soul."

"You fucker!" Orion punched him in the arm before dragging him close for a hug. "You had me fooled."

"I had to if I wanted them to ignore me. Now, what do you say we go help our mate?"

"Fuck yeah, and after we do, I'm burning this hellhole down," Orion vowed because some places should never exist.

CHAPTER 18

A FEW HOURS BEFORE ADELINE WENT TO THE RESCUE...

When Charon, Adeline's grim reaper daddy, mentioned she had a brother, her first reaction was "yay, family."

"What can you tell me about my brother?" she'd eagerly asked.

"Not much. Unlike you, he managed to keep his power under control enough that I never realized he existed, but while careful, he apparently slipped up enough that the same people seeking you out managed to capture him."

Adeline took a second to digest this before saying, "He's a prisoner?"

"Yes. Your brother has been held captive for years."

"So why didn't you do anything to save him?" she asked. After all, he'd created a safe place for her.

"I cannot act since he is hidden somewhere even I can't detect."

"If that's the case, then how can you know he's the one yanking souls?"

The cowl practically dripped with disdain as he said, "Because you and your brother are the only *anima dissecuerit* at the moment, and I had confirmation. Someone who worked there died, and their soul was quite talkative when I fetched it. It claimed they were forcing your brother to sunder souls."

"And did that soul not tell you where to find them?"

"It did." The cloak stilled. "However, whoever is in charge is crafty and had already relocated by the time I arrived."

"Surely they left a clue?" she insisted.

"A burnt shell was all that remained. However, it is my belief, given your recent encounters with *immortui*, that they are probably somewhere in or around this city. We must locate their headquarters to put an end to the sundering."

"Okay, so the plan is to find the bad guy's lair and rescue my brother. Sounds doable. Where do we start looking?"

"There is no we. I cannot interfere in human affairs."

"You interfered with me," she interjected.

"A momentary lapse of judgment," his dry reply.

"Not going to get a Father's Day card at this rate," she quipped.

"Never asked to be a father."

"Well, you are one, so suck it up, grim buttercup. How can I help my brother since you're not willing?"

"As mentioned, you need to locate and then extract him from their custody."

"Oh, just that. I mean, sure, piece of cake. I'll just wander the city aimlessly because I'm sure they've got a great big sign that says Soul Stealers Inc. out front to make it easy. And then let's say I do find it. I should what, just ask for my brother? I'm sure they'll hand him over, no fuss or muss." Yeah, it might have been a tad snippy, but seriously, could he not see the insanity of his request?

"Should you discover the headquarters and get inside, you will call upon me for assistance."

She blinked. "I'm confused. You said like two seconds ago that you weren't helping."

"This wouldn't be help but rather me correcting the balance of things. The sundered souls aren't entering the Styx, causing an imbalance that requires correction."

"When you say correct, do you mean you're going kill everyone who was involved?"

"Yes."

"Seems kind of harsh." She couldn't have said why she argued other than he'd annoyed her with his stand-offish attitude.

"These kinds of transgressions require severe measures."

"It's murder," of which she'd be abetting.

"It will benefit the universe."

"If you say so, Father."

"Don't call me that," he grumbled.

For a guy with no feelings, she'd touched a nerve. "Any suggestions on how I'm supposed to find this supposed lair?" Because despite the danger, she would because Orion needed her, and she had a sneaky feeling Ambrose did as well.

"If I knew the location, we wouldn't be having this discussion."

"I don't know how you expect me to find it."

"The fates will provide." A cryptic answer that had her gnashing her teeth.

Meow. Smudge eyed the door to the shop, and Adeline ignored her dad to check since Smudge wasn't one to talk without reason.

"Fudge!" she exclaimed, seeing him through the glass. She opened the door to let him in, and her kitty actually rubbed against her legs before choosing to twine his tail with Smudge's. She dropped down to pet him, crooning, "Where have you been? I was so worried."

Meow. Mew. Miauo. Rowr.

Her cat spoke, and Adeline nodded, pretending she understood.

Meanwhile, turned out Daddy Charon could speak feline. "He says he knows where they've taken the hounds. The place is heavily guarded by human soldiers, and the building is comprised of lead and iron, which explains why it's been undetectable."

"Did Fudge happen to give you an address?"

"Cats don't deal in those kinds of specifics, but perhaps he recalls some landmarks."

Charon crouched, and while he didn't say anything audible, her cat began talking as if replying.

Mew. Miaw. Mo. Mo. Meow.

Charon nodded his hooded head and stood. "On his return journey, he passed a giant green barrel on legs, as well as drank some milk from a cow. He also said something about a sign showing giant teeth."

It took her a minute before she slowly said, "Sounds like he came from the east of town. The green barrel on legs has to be the water tower. There's farms out that way as well. I guess we have a direction to look, but the problem is getting there. I don't have a car or cash for an Uber, and it will take forever on foot."

Keeble popped in to clear his throat. "Master Charon, we've prepared a countering tea for the lady."

"Excellent."

"What is countering tea?" she questioned.

"A beverage to annul the effects of the dulling one. If you're going to confront those using your brother, you should have your full abilities to draw on."

"By abilities, you mean the accident-causing thing." She bit her lower lip before adding, "You expect me to kill people."

"If necessary, yes. Or would you prefer to be taken captive and used like your brother?"

Her mouth opened and shut. "Good point. Any

clues on how to use my power?" A strange thing to ask given she'd always thought of herself as human.

"There is no time to teach, so I would suggest letting your emotions act for you."

"Weird advice from the guy with none."

He spoke as if she hadn't. "Once you are inside the building, I cannot enter without an invitation."

"What are you, part vampire?"

"Grims aren't a part of this world and cannot go where we please without taking a corporeal form."

"You're here right now."

"Because Keeble invited me."

"If you can't come without an invite, then how are you supposed to collect souls?"

"If they don't get lost, then they are gathered from the Styx."

"Didn't you also say you gather them from me? I never invited you to my apartment."

"No, but your feline companions did."

"Oh." Her lips pursed. Knowing her pets were more than just cats would be something to unpack later. "Once inside, how do I contact you? You said this place is shielded. How will you hear me?"

"You are of my flesh. If you call, I will come."

Okay, that was creepy and kind of daddy-ish all at once. "Assuming I can find this place. A few landmarks aren't an exact location."

"Listen to your instincts and you will prevail."

His final words before he left in a swirl of shadow, which had her blinking at the sudden brightness. She pondered everything she'd learned. The fact she was half grim reaper. Had a brother. Could kill people. *Had* killed people. She felt kind of bad. Turned out she had been right about being bad luck after all.

Would she have to worry about hurting Orion and Ambrose? Maybe she should wait to fret about that once she rescued them.

She eyed her cats. "You guys coming?"

Meow. She took that as a yes.

Keeble brought out a new mug. "Drink up."

She eyed the bright green fluid. "How quickly does it work?"

"As soon as it hits your belly. Quick now, your ride is on its way."

Ride? Right after she finished her tea, a sedan pulled up, the windows blacked out, the interior sleek and new. The driver turned out to be a faun named Seamus who happened to know the location of the billboard when she described it.

As they passed it on the single-lane highway, she peered out the windows, wondering what Charon meant when he said listen to her instincts. What instincts? How would she—

The sudden dizzy spell had her muttering, "Take the next turn."

"Yes, ma'am," grunted Seamus.

The two-lane driveway, framed by trees, led to a large but only half-full parking lot and a multi-story structure with no business sign on the outside. She knew she'd found the spot, though, by the snipers on the roof and the same soldiers patrolling the perimeter of the building.

She could have marched right inside. However, she decided to be smart. Rather than hand herself over, she offered Seamus some cash to bring them a deal.

Her in exchange for Ambrose and Orion.

The reply took only a few minutes.

Seamus clomped back out, exclaiming, "They said yes."

"Really?" She'd expected to have to negotiate more.

"The woman in charge said they'll be along shortly. Once they exit, you're supposed to hand yourself over."

This moved faster than expected. "Promise you'll take Ambrose and Orion somewhere safe."

"What about you, ma'am?"

Her lips flattened. "I need to put a stop to what's going on here."

And rescue her brother.

CHAPTER 19

After Adeline had Seamus make the offer, it took almost twenty minutes before the doors to the building opened and soldiers spilled out, forming a wall, but with them... Ambrose and Orion. The former stood stiffly, staring straight ahead. The latter had been muffled and his hands tied behind his back.

Adeline stood with her cats, taking deep breaths to calm her nerves. Charon had told her to call him when she entered. She would. However, first she wanted to meet the people who'd thought it okay to medically experiment by stealing souls. Did she think they'd have a good excuse? Nope. However, she did want to hear it.

Her walk across that parking lot had her itching. She remained all too aware of the snipers on the roof. The closer she drew to the soldiers, the more nervous she became. It didn't help that her prickling now had nausea added to it. A sense of wrongness oozed from the building. How did no one else notice it?

Orion's gaze smoldered with anger—and worry. His eyes yelled at her: *You idiot, why did you come?* As if she would leave him captive. She might not have known him for long, but she felt things. A sense of connection and rightness that deserved exploring. She couldn't do that if he remained captive, or worse...

As for Ambrose, his blank stare terrified. She was too late. They'd taken his—

He winked. Just once, but the tension in her eased at the realization he pretended to be soulless. Most likely hoping for the element of surprise. Smart.

Knowing he played possum eased something in her. Made her believe things might just work out.

She glanced down at her kitties. "You two get the boys to safety."

Smudge made a noise.

"I know you want to come, but I have to do this alone."

With that, she walked past the boys and entered the lair of... She had no name for the bad guys. Not even any faces either. The soldiers wore their armor and helmets. Even once in the building, she saw nothing to really identify who ran the place or what they did. They really should get a logo. Maybe a scythe or a cloaked figure.

A soldier by an elevator beckoned. "You're expected upstairs."

"By who?" she asked.

"The doctor. This way." Again, he gestured.

A doctor? Weren't those in the medical profession supposed to preserve life?

The elevator didn't suddenly seal or do anything funky. Apparently, that happened only in movies. Instead, it simply went up, and Adeline exited into an office space lit by fluorescents because twilight had given way to night.

"They're in the boardroom." The soldier pointed, and she headed for the door set inside a wall of glass. Through it, she could see a large table surrounded by chairs and more people than expected.

She entered, and her gaze darted to take in those present—most in military uniform, a few in suits—but her gaze zeroed in on the woman in a white coat.

"Adeline Gagnon. About time we met." The woman eyed her in an analytical manner that made Adeline want to slap her.

"Who are you? What is this place?" Adeline asked. And what did the military have to do with it?

"We don't have a name, as we prefer to keep a low profile, but suffice it to say, we are a group of humans looking to halt the creep of cryptids. I am Doctor Monroe."

"The psycho stealing souls," Adeline stated then added, "Why? Why would you do that?"

"Because I can." Dr. Monroe's lips quirked as if it were funny. "Because souls are the most powerful form of energy there is."

"To do what?"

"That's a secret, I'm afraid. Suffice it to say, this ability we've harnessed will change how wars are conducted. How we age. Souls are the key to everything."

"What you're doing is killing people."

"Nobodies." She waved a hand as if they didn't matter.

"I thought doctors weren't supposed to do harm," Adeline remarked.

"No harm to humans. Cryptids don't count." The doctor offered a cold smile.

"I'm sure they'd disagree."

A man in uniform with short-cropped hair barked, "It's about time the monsters were reminded that humans are the master race."

The comment made Adeline recoil. "That's a horrible thing to say."

"It's the truth," he insisted. "For too long, we've allowed them to spread and spawn. It's time we took back our world. I'm finally in a position where I have access to the cryptid secrets and the ability to shield our actions until we're ready to eradicate them from this planet."

"You're talking about genocide."

"To protect mankind," he boasted, as if he weren't talking about killing entire species.

"What does this have to do with me?"

Dr. Monroe replied. "It's come to our attention that you might have an interesting genealogy. Did your mother perchance speak to you of your father?"

"My mother died when I was young."

"She also lied about her true identity. You knew her as Bethany Gagnon, but in reality, her name was Jessica Long. She worked with me on a project decades ago that suffered an unfortunate setback," Monroe stated. "Thankfully, she survived the mishap, or you wouldn't have been born."

Had Adeline not talked to Charon, the shock would have hit harder. "And what was her job for this project?"

"Carrying you. She was a surrogate, her egg fertilized with semen from a unique and rare entity. You've probably heard of grim reapers."

"They're not real," Adeline claimed to see what Monroe would spill.

"Oh, they exist, just not usually in a shape we can touch. However, they can apparently take a solid form if they choose. With careful planning and some luck, we managed to capture one and get samples. Through some very intricate process, we managed to create two viable embryos. Your mother carried one."

"And the other?" Adeline asked, wanting to get as much info as possible before this depraved lunatic died.

"He's downstairs in his room. Would you like to meet Thaddeus?"

Her brother's name was Thaddeus. She couldn't stop an excited, "Yes, please."

"You will, but only after we run some tests. Given

you never appeared on our radar before now, I have to wonder if you inherited any of your father's reaping ability. You might have escaped us entirely if you'd not attracted the soulless who'd escaped. When we relocated here, we wondered where they kept running off to. We couldn't bring them outside the building for any training lest they disappear." Monroe dared to complain.

"So you're the reason they kept showing up at my door."

"We wouldn't have lost so many if you'd reported them," she accused.

Adeline shrugged. "Didn't want to deal with the paperwork." She paused before saying, "You sent that kraken to find me."

"Given its ability to travel the sewers and squeeze into small holes, we thought it the best for hunting down your location. Only its tracker failed to emit a signal until it emerged."

"It almost killed me."

"Which would have been unfortunate," Monroe said flatly, no hint of remorse.

Adeline tired of the word games. "You know, Charon is still pissed at what you did to him."

"How do you know his name?" Monroe narrowed her gaze.

"We recently met."

"When? Where?" the military fellow with the brush cut barked, rising from the table.

"Sit down, Harry. We're safe in this building. You

know I had it shielded. Even if I killed someone right now, no grim reaper can enter." Monroe huffed.

"Are you sure about that?" Adeline asked.

"Don't you even think to play games. You are in my control, and by now, so are the men you traded yourself for," Monroe threatened.

"Orion and Ambrose? Yeah, I doubt very much you managed to capture them twice. And even if you did, your reign of soul stealing ends today."

Adeline didn't wait to hear a rebuttal but shouted with her mind. *Hey, Father, if you're listening, I'm with the ringleader of this operation. I'd love it if you joined me.*

No reply, but the room suddenly darkened. Shadows filled the corners and coalesced into a looming form atop the boardroom table.

Monroe gaped. Everyone did.

Monroe gasped, "You can't be here. No one died."

"I was invited by my daughter," Charon's low shivery reply.

"Shoot him!" the military guy yelled. The soldiers obeyed, the muzzles of their guns flashing as they all fired at once. A rapid fire barrage of bullets that passed right through Adeline's dad.

"My turn," Charon said when the shooting stopped. He held out his arm, the sleeve falling away from his bony hand. In a timbre most terrible, he said, "For your crimes against the natural order, your souls are forfeit."

The last syllable hadn't even faded when the screaming started.

CHAPTER 20

The elevator appeared caught on the second floor, the same spot Ambrose and Orion had been taken to meet with the doctor and other folks.

An impatient Orion didn't want to wait. "Take the stairs?"

Ambrose didn't hesitate. "Yeah. They're to the left."

As they jogged to the door, the cats slipped past them and bounded up the steps.

Let them scout ahead. Ambrose followed as Orion huffed, "I can't believe you faked being a zombie."

"If I hadn't, I might have ended up one." He still couldn't believe the man in that locked room let him go, admonishing him to not break character at all until he felt certain he could make his move.

"You could have told me," Orion sulked.

"I had to make it believable."

"Oh, I believed it all right, asshole." Orion slapped him on the back. "Glad I don't have to smash in your head, bro."

"Me too." Because it had been close.

The doctor left the room after instructing Thaddeus to do his thing. The guy in the chair stared at Ambrose for a moment.

"You have a silver soul," Thaddeus said.

"If you say so." Ambrose couldn't do much strapped to the gurney.

The man rose and stood over him, his eyes shadowed. "Silver usually means god-touched. Do you serve a god?"

"The Goddess Hekate. I am her scion."

"You know what Dr. Monroe wants me to do," the man said.

"You're the one who's been taking people's souls."

"I have," Thaddeus admitted softly. "But not because I want to."

"I can help you escape," Ambrose offered.

"Can you? Because I've given up hope. They keep me locked in here, night and day. I'm tested daily, my blood drawn. Everything about me measured. I swear they'd spy on me every second if they could, but something about me makes their cameras fail." The man offered a faint smile. "It's the reason why we can speak right now."

"Release me and I'll get us out of here."

"One man alone can't do it. But if you were to escape and bring help..."

"I can do that, but I'll need my soul."

"Obviously," Thaddeus' wry reply. "But we'll need to convince Monroe that I've taken it. You need to act like one of the soulless. No expression. Just listless movement. Oh, and you'll need to scream."

"Why scream?" Ambrose asked.

"Because taking a soul hurts." The man's lips turned down. "It's torture of the cruelest order."

And so Ambrose shrieked. Screamed like that time as a boy when the saloon owner thought he wasn't washing dishes fast enough and whipped him for it.

Monroe entered after a bit, took one look, and murmured, "Excellent. I wondered if it would work with a deity-blessed subject."

"You're taking a risk pissing off a god," her captive replied.

"I can handle a god. Rest up. You'll be doing his companion shortly."

"I said no more," Thaddeus grumbled. "I'm tired."

"One more and then I'll allow you to watch a movie."

Monroe had Ambrose escorted with only a pair of soldiers back to his cage. He'd debated breaking free at that point; however, he couldn't leave Orion behind. So he returned to that wretched chamber and managed to hold on to the ruse, even as he felt horrible for putting Orion through such anguish. But it worked. When the time came to act, the soldiers never saw his fist coming.

But they'd not won yet.

The stairs didn't take long to climb at a jog. The cats waited for them at the door to the second-floor landing. They heard the screams the moment they exited the stairwell.

A man yelled, "No! No! I swear I—" Abrupt silence followed.

They entered to find the oddest sight. A figure dressed in a flowing cloak pointed a skeletal hand at the people gathered. Each time he aimed a finger, a person went wide-eyed and died. Instantly.

"Holy fuck, is that a grim reaper?" Orion whispered. Not something either of them had ever seen before.

Ambrose chose to ignore the specter of death to seek out Adeline. He caught a glimpse of her as she went through a door.

"This way," he yelled to Orion. They fled across the room only to find the door locked.

"We need a keycard," Orion stated before adding, "Give me a second." He strode over to the General sidling for the exit and snatched the card clipped to his jacket.

"Hey," he yelled. "Give it back."

"I don't think so."

The General lunged for Orion, only to pause before connecting. His mouth opened. His eyes widened. And over he keeled.

For a second, Ambrose worried as Orion's gaze met that of the Grim Reaper.

To his surprise, the cloaked figure inclined his hooded head and said, "Go find her."

Orion strode back to Ambrose and shook the card. "Got one."

They slapped it on the security screen and, when the door beeped, slipped through it to find a smaller set of stairs that went up and down.

Their noses led them to descend, the patter of Adeline's feet a faraway echo.

They descended further than the prison basement, the last landing blocked by a door that required keycard access. Adeline stood in front of the door with her hands planted on her hips.

She whirled to exclaim, "She's getting away."

No need to ask who. Dr. Monroe had been the only one missing from the chaos above.

"I've got this." Ambrose slapped the card on the reader, and the moment the door beeped, Adeline entered.

They found themselves in a lab, a massive one with machines Ambrose couldn't identify but had seen the last time he'd passed through.

"The doctor is most likely hiding out with the man in the solitary cell," he whispered to Orion.

"Why is he here instead of the cages?" Orion replied.

"He's the one who's been taking souls."

Adeline already stood in front of the only locked door and stamped her foot impatiently.

Ambrose neared and murmured, "Why don't you stand aside and let us handle this, sweetheart?"

"No thanks. This concerns me more than you," she stated.

Fair enough. Ambrose unlocked the door, and Adeline walked in and halted. Ambrose shadowed her and moved to the left, while Orion flanked her right. Inside the room, the man he'd seen before remained seated in his chair. Short dark hair, shoulders broad, arms muscled. Thaddeus might be a prisoner but he kept fit.

Dr. Monroe stood by his side with a smirk, holding a remote similar to the one they'd found on the soldier's tool belt.

"I see you misled me, Thaddeus. You were supposed to take his soul," Monroe chided. "That will teach me for thinking you'd learned your lesson when it comes to obeying."

Thaddeus ducked his head.

"Leave him alone," Adeline huffed. "It's over."

"Oh no it's not. You see, the Grim Reaper can't hurt me. I'm protected," Monroe declared, pulling an amulet out from her shirt. "This prevents him and Thaddeus from yanking my soul. Soon, my scientists will know how to replicate it, and all of humanity will be shielded, making it easy for us to pick off the cryptids."

"You sick bitch," Orion breathed, taking a step forward.

Monroe snapped. "I don't listen to dogs. Thaddeus, take their souls."

"No." The man spoke softly but firmly.

"Are you really going to defy me?" She pressed the button, and Thaddeus fell out of the chair, writhing. Well, that explained the remote's use.

Adeline stepped forward. "It's over, Dr. Monroe. You can't escape."

"Who's going to stop me? You?" The woman laughed and pressed the button on her remote again. This time it wasn't just Thaddeus who hit the ground writhing. Orion and Ambrose joined him. As Ambrose jiggled in agony, Monroe boasted, "The first thing I do with a new specimen is give them the controlling chip."

"I don't need them to knock you out." Adeline raised her fists, however, Monroe remained one step ahead and pulled out a small revolver.

"Pity I have to shoot you. But at least I'll have your DNA to play with."

He could see Adeline struggle with the realization she'd die. Fear should have been the reaction, but instead, he saw anger.

"The only one dying is you." As Adeline said it, a strange thing happened. A chain reaction, that began with Thaddeus crawling for his chair but knocking it over, which hit a side table that held a pitcher of water. The fluid hit the floor and ran, pooling under Monroe's feet, which was when a light suspended from the ceiling suddenly came crashing down, spitting out sparks of electricity before hitting the puddle.

It didn't take long for the electrocution to send

Monroe to the floor, gazing sightlessly, the gun falling from her limp fingers.

By a fluke, they'd won the fight. It would seem the amulet didn't have a clause to prevent accidents.

Before they could celebrate, the room filled with a shadow.

Uh-oh. The Grim Reaper had arrived.

CHAPTER 21

THE ADRENALINE PROVED SLOW TO LEAVE ADELINE. THE sight of her brother and lovers writhing in agony had filled Adeline with pulsing anger. Remembering what Charon had told her, she let it consume her and explode.

The chain reaction proved almost comical.

The result? Monroe died. Adeline actually saw the woman's soul leave her body, a yellow and green amorphous shape that soon pulled itself into a more recognizable form.

The sudden darkness in the room distracted her as Charon arrived with his always-moving cloak.

"Hello, Father. You're a tad too late," Adeline stated, proud of herself for having put a stop to the horrible woman.

"Just in time, actually. I see a soul in need of gathering," Charon murmured, which led to Monroe, now fully formed, quivering. Gone was her cocky expression as fear tugged her features.

"Stay away from me," Monroe huffed.

"Now, Felicia, is that any way to greet an old lover?" Charon purred. "How nice to see you again. You left before I could say goodbye the last time."

"I can't be dead." Monroe clutched at her neck, only the amulet she'd worn didn't follow her in death. "This protects my soul from the likes of you and your grim spawn."

"From us directly taking, yes," Charon agreed. "However, accidents are accidents."

"Stay away from me." Monroe backed away, her gaze flitting side to side as she sought escape.

"I can't do that, Felicia. It's my duty to bring your soul to its next incarnation. I'm thinking perhaps an insect, something easily squashed or eaten. Or maybe a rabbit or mouse, always running and hiding from predators."

"No. You can't do this to me. I bested you." Monroe stamped her foot.

"You did, and then my daughter beat you. Ironic, isn't it?" Charon declared. "Enough chatting. Time to go. I've got several souls that need reassignment." At his words, his cloak rippled, and Adeline would have sworn she saw faces pressing through the fabric.

The soul of Dr. Monroe tried to flee, but the scythe, seen in lore, finally emerged. Charon reached with the blade and snared Monroe. He dragged her into his embrace, his cloak enveloping her thoroughly.

Charon's hood faced Adeline for a moment then turned towards the collapsed form of his son. "One more thing to clean up..." He held out his hand, and she saw as the souls clinging to her brother separated from him, flitting to Charon before disappearing. When the flow stopped, Charon reached for Thaddeus, saying, "Your turn."

Adeline threw herself between them. "You can't kill my brother."

"I should. I should remove you both. It is dangerous to leave you alive. Him, especially."

"He only did what they forced him to do. He won't use his powers like that anymore," Adeline swore even as she'd never once spoken to Thaddeus. But surely he deserved a chance?

"He'd better not. You either. Or I will return..." With that grim announcement, Charon disappeared, and as the light returned, Adeline found herself first in one bone-crushing hug then another.

"What happened? Are you okay? What was that you said to the Grim Reaper?" Ambrose exclaimed.

"Yeah, I'm fine." She'd have to explain her grim daddy later. First... she moved to her brother's side. Thaddeus sat up with a wary expression on his face.

"Hi." She dropped to her haunches and held out her hand. "I'm Adeline."

"You said you were my sister."

She nodded. "And that creepy guy you just saw is our dad, Charon."

He grimaced. "About as warm as the doctors in this place."

"I think that actually was for him, or we'd both be dead. You ready to bust out of this joint?"

Thaddeus nodded yes, only to then shake no. "I shouldn't be out in the world. He's right. I'm dangerous."

"Actually, I know of a tea to help with that."

"Tea?"

She grinned. "Made by elves. But I swear it tastes good."

"I have nowhere to go."

"Yes, you do. You have a place with me." She held out her hand. "How do you feel about making sandwiches?"

He appeared confused but took her grip and stood. "I haven't made a sandwich in a long time."

"That's okay. I'll teach you," Adeline offered.

"Can we leave this place? It's giving me the creeps," Orion declared.

"Yes, but first we have to do one more thing."

They freed the prisoners with souls, but unfortunately, nothing could be done for those who had been sundered, which led to Thaddeus weeping. "I had no choice."

"I know," she replied softly. It was too easy to imagine their roles reversed had she been caught. She would have done the same to avoid torture. Besides, she couldn't claim any better, given she'd been accidentally using her power to take souls from the living.

Calling them accidents didn't change the fact those people died because of her.

Once they'd cleared the place of captives, they torched the building, a fire being the only way of ensuring everything got destroyed. Everything but the two prizes of the project.

Seamus drove them back to the city, where Ambrose rented a hotel suite with two bedrooms, a living room, and even a small kitchen. The cats took off to explore right away.

Thaddeus stared for a good minute before whispering, "It feels like a dream. I'm afraid I'll wake up."

Adeline put an arm around him and murmured, "You're free now. Have a hot shower. Order some room service. Watch some boob tube."

"A hot shower..." He sighed. "That sounds like heaven."

It did, which was why Adeline headed for the second bedroom, saying, "I need to wash off."

In short order, Orion and Ambrose joined her.

Naked.

She shook a finger at them. "We don't have time for that. Thaddeus probably shouldn't be alone."

"Your brother's gone to bed. I gave him a little something to sleep," Ambrose stated.

"You drugged him?" she exclaimed.

"Magicked him at his wish and with Hekate's help. He said he wanted a chance to rest, but his emotions were making that too difficult. And before you panic about him being alone, the cats are with him."

Her shoulders relaxed. "Sorry if I went all sister bear for a second. I feel bad for him. His life in that place could have easily been mine."

"You going to explain about your brother and that grim reaper who showed up to help?" Orion asked, soaping his hands to run over her body.

She sighed. "So, it turns out I'm not entirely human. Or cryptid. And that grim reaper you saw, that's my daddy, Charon." She explained about the sandwich shop and the experiment, a bomb of shocking information that most people would have needed time to process, maybe even a break to see if they could handle it.

What did Orion say? "Fucking cool."

She blinked wet lashes at him. "Um, not really. My half-blood is the reason why I used to have problems with freak accidents. It was my soul-taking ability manifesting. I'm a killer."

"So am I," Orion scoffed. "Not a big deal."

"It is if I don't want to accidentally kill people."

"You just need to learn how to use it."

"Use it?" she squeaked.

Ambrose was the one to nod. "Yes, use it for good. There's a lot of evil in the world."

"My father warned us against utilizing our ability," she reminded.

"Your father would have killed you if he didn't want you to have it. I know a bit about Charon. He's never been one to care before. But he obviously cared enough to give you a safe space."

Her nose wrinkled. "I guess."

"I'm more worried about us," Orion declared. "Your daddy's the Grim Reaper. What if he decides he doesn't like the dirty things we're about to do to his daughter?"

The statement widened her eyes but also shot tingles through her. "What kind of things?"

Orion grinned. "Ambrose, what do you say we show her?"

They dried off quickly, her hands trembling slightly in anticipation. Was she ready for this? She barely knew these men, and yet she couldn't deny her desire or the feelings she had for them. Feelings she wanted to explore.

Ambrose drew her into his arms for a kiss, while Orion pressed against her back, his lips dragging over the back of her neck. When they whirled her, it was his mouth then claiming hers, while Orion gripped her hips and nibbled her shoulder.

They ended up on the bed, her flat on her back, the men on their hands and knees on either side. There was something visually titillating about the way their faces hovered over her breasts. As if synchronized, they latched onto her erect nipples, their hot mouths tugging, sucking, teasing. It had her gasping and writhing at the dual sensation.

Theirs hands roamed, stroking her flesh, skimming over her curves, leaving her aware of her body in a way that made everything more intense. Someone's fingers, she didn't know whose, teased her between her thighs, the fingertips lightly tickling her nether lips.

"I need a taste," Orion growled.

"Then go ahead," Ambrose offered. "I can wait."

"I have a better idea," Orion slyly stated. "Flip over, sweetheart."

She chose to not ask why and rolled to her stomach then squeaked as hands tugged her onto her hands and knees.

"Give her your cock," a raspy Orion ordered.

"What do you say sweetheart?" Ambrose actually asked, despite the fact his erect dick bobbed mere inches from her lips.

She showed Ambrose by taking his thick cock into her mouth, her mouth gliding over the silky skin. Then almost biting down as Orion blew hotly on her sex.

"Don't you stop sucking," Orion purred against her trembling flesh.

She bobbed her head a few strokes before pausing as Orion began to lick her, his tongue parting her lips, teasing her, making her forget everything but passion.

Ambrose threaded his fingers in her hair and helped guide her, his hips lightly thrusting, and she took it all, grunting and moaning around his cock as Orion flicked her clit. He lay under her, eating her, his fingers slipping in to give her something to clamp.

Ambrose groaned. "Fuck me, this is intense."

Intense didn't begin to describe it.

She inhaled the cock in her mouth harder, and Ambrose replied by pumping his hips faster. Orion matched their frenzied pace, and she tightened, readying to come when he stopped.

"Time to feel you come on my cock," Orion stated.

He positioned himself behind her, and while she sucked, he fucked. Literally. He slid his long cock into her, and she keened. Oh my. *Oh...*

It was almost too much, getting it from two ends, the cock between her lips thickening, and pulsing, the one in her pussy stretching her.

She lost her rhythm and could only moan.

As Orion fucked, his hand slid under to tease her clit, rubbing it. She couldn't hold on. Her channel clenched and then rippled as her orgasm hit and rolled.

"That's it, sweetheart. Come for me." Orion dug his fingers into her cheeks as he kept thrusting. Pushing deep, drawing out the pleasure.

When he finally slowed, his voice was husky when he said, "Your turn."

Ambrose shook his head. "I'm too close to creaming. It won't be any fun for her."

"That's what you think," Orion murmured. "Ambrose, lie on your back. Sweetheart, I want you to ride him, reverse cowgirl style."

"What?" She blinked, still bemused by her pleasure.

"Like this." Orion's hands guided her so that she straddled Ambrose, but facing away. Ambrose's hands clamped around her waist, and he began to bounce her, drawing gasps from her.

The pleasure reignited, and she moaned as she enjoyed the penetration from another angle.

"Lean back, sweetheart, just a bit," Orion whispered.

She braced her hands and angled as asked, wondering why, until she felt hot breath on her pussy. A glance down showed Orion between her thighs, and Ambrose's. His mouth latched onto her clit, already sensitive and needy.

He lapped and sucked while Ambrose ground into her. The dual sweet spots making her shudder. And to her surprise, a second orgasm struck, fast and hard, her pussy tightening so hard around Ambrose he shouted.

"Fuck me, I'm coming."

They both were. A dual climax that wrung them dry and left them panting.

It was the best sex she'd ever had.

Nestled between their bodies, she sighed. So this was happiness? Definitely better than a book, although she could have done without the reality of cats who chose to meow at her nonstop when dawn crested because they wanted food.

But she forgave them because, turned out, she didn't mind the breakfast sausage she got served.

EPILOGUE

Being the mate of hounds—or as Orion teasingly called her, mistress—turned out to be amazing. The lovemaking, the cuddling, the way they made her feel special every single day. But more than that, she no longer felt alone.

A good thing she'd found her mates since her cats abandoned her, AKA got reassigned. She might have been miffed, only it turned out they'd been sent to take care of her brother. She found out in the oddest way. She received potted flowers, an incredible lush bouquet, that came with a note.

Dearest Adeline,

I am delighted to see you helped vanquish the blight on my land. Also thank you for taking care of Cole and Fiona, whom you know as Fudge and Smudge. Now that their services are no longer needed, they are being reassigned, but fear not, it is to someone you know. I think your brother could use some feline friends on his upcoming journey given his story isn't yet done.

Enjoy your new life. May it be as fruitful as my land.
Sincerely,
Mother Earth.

Adeline might have been a tad more impressed at *the* Earth goddess contacting her if she'd not met Hekate first. The goddess had literally transported her to some otherworldly throne room, where she thanked Adeline personally for taking care of her boys. Asked her if she'd like to be included on future tasks, and then gave Adeline an amulet to use to stifle her power instead of the daily tea. She gave one to Thaddeus as well, although he chose to keep drinking the stuff as if fearful it would fail.

Given they'd moved to New York—because it turned out her boys had a gorgeous place overlooking the skyline with a guest suite for her brother—she had to quit her job. The sandwich shop remained open, under new management, as Keeble and his crew took it over from Charon.

As for her grim daddy? It had been three months since the events with Monroe and her secret facility and Adeline thought she'd never see him again until the living room grew suddenly dark.

Charon appeared, his cloak just as undulating and shadowy as before, but his voice was soft when he said without greeting, "I am going to be a grandfather."

"Wait, what?" was her reply. She glanced at her flat belly.

"She will be special. Very special. So be sure to guard her closely."

And then, to her surprise, skeletal fingers, which felt like flesh, stroked her cheek. "Be happy, daughter. I find myself oddly interested in your well-being."

With that, Charon left, and when the boys found her, she had a bemused expression.

"What's up, sweetheart?" Orion flopped beside her on the couch.

"I'm pregnant."

Ambrose tripped and landed on his ass.

She smiled as she added, "It's a girl."

"Yahoo!" Orion yelled, jumping to his feet. "She's gonna be her daddies' princess."

"She'll be too cute given our genetics. We'll have to invest in a property with a tall fence," a somber Ambrose declared.

"Electrified," Orion added.

"With spikes to prevent boys from climbing over."

"Or they could and then I'll bite their ass for trying to mess with our girl," Orion eagerly stated.

Ambrose nodded. "We won't let anyone like you date her."

"Agreed." Orion bobbed his own head. "Nothing but the best for our daughter."

Our.

Adeline looked at her two mates, the three of them forming a triangle that would never break—and always be fun in the bedroom, hence why she crooked her finger and said, "Shall we celebrate?"

She was proud to say she made them both howl. Twice.

THADDEUS CLUTCHED the amulet given to him by the Goddess Hekate. It helped quite a bit when it came to not noticing or craving the souls around him. They teased him at every turn. It would be so easy to snatch one. He had never admitted it aloud, but he enjoyed touching people's souls.

His sister might believe him to be good, but he knew better. It didn't help his addiction that souls kept flocking to him after death. The way they filled him with warmth. Made him feel stronger, at least for a moment before he called upon Charon to transfer them to the Styx.

Not his first choice, but he'd sworn to Charon he wouldn't be stealing or keeping stray souls anymore. Every time his father visited to remove those he inadvertently attracted, he offered a stern warning.

"Remember, I let you live on the condition you do no evil."

Which felt kind of broad in scope. Who defined evil? How would he recognize it? Did that mean if he encountered it he should act?

He'd have sworn the plant on the kitchen counter whispered with its rustling leaves, *You will soon find out.*

Smudge glanced at him with bright green eyes that flared and remained bright as the cat transformed suddenly into a woman with dark and silver-streaked hair.

"What the fuck? I thought you were a cat!" he exclaimed.

"Only because I was undercover. Name is Fiona." She smiled slyly at him. "And you heard the Earth Goddess. Sounds like we're going on an adventure."

WHAT DO YOU SAY, SHOULD WE FIND OUT WHAT HAPPENS TO THADDEUS IN *EARTH'S REAPER*?

www.ingramcontent.com/pod-product-compliance
Lightning Source LLC
LaVergne TN
LVHW031540060526
838200LV00056B/4581